Ryan was the one who always came to her rescue

Once more, Lockett would be running off into the unknown on the back of Ryan's motorcycle. The irony of it almost knocked her over. Carefully, she gathered up her skirts before he picked her up and hoisted her over his shoulder.

"Do we have to do it this way?" she asked, bumping and thumping as he maneuvered them out the window.

"It's the only way I can climb and carry you at the same time," he muttered, amid yards of tulle. Lockett squeezed her eyes closed. This had seemed a lot more romantic at seventeen.

Finally, when they were on his motorcycle, her veil floating behind her and sixteen yards of satin and lace blowing in the breeze, they roared off into the sun.

"It appears there won't be a wedding today," Lockett said cheerfully.

ABOUT THE AUTHOR

Julie Kistler loved the idea of being part of our For Richer, For Poorer trilogy since she's always wanted to be a pampered heiress and she's always loved dark and dangerous men. She has each side of the tracks meet here with enough sexy banter to fuel Ryan's motorcycle! She lives in central Illinois with her tall, dark and handsome husband.

Books by Julie Kistler

HARLEQUIN AMERICAN ROMANCE

JULIE KISTLER

RYAN'S BRIDE

Harlequin Books

TORONTO • NEW YORK • LONDON
AMSTERDAM • PARIS • SYDNEY • HAMBURG
STOCKHOLM • ATHENS • TOKYO • MILAN
MADRID • WARSAW • BUDAPEST • AUCKLAND

ISBN 0-373-16575-7

RYAN'S BRIDE

Copyright © 1995 by Julie Kistler.

Printed in U.S.A.

Chapter One

The Passionate Pirate

Lockett Kensington was in the midst of a terrible evening.

"Lockett, you'd better be enjoying my party," Tish Bingwell said petulantly. She handed Lockett another tall, cool drink, this one a pale peach color with a tiger lily for a swizzle stick. "I have a surprise for later, and I certainly hope everybody appreciates it. It cost a fortune."

The Bingwells had more money than Croesus, but it didn't keep Tish from accounting for each dime.

"The party's lovely," Lockett assured her. She set the glass down next to the piña colada and the daiquiri she'd barely touched.

She still wasn't quite sure what to make of this "bachelorette party," but it certainly was different. The theme was tropical, for no reason Lockett could discern, with garlands of orchids and passion flowers positively overpowering Tish's elegant suburban living room and terrace.

Tish had clearly decided that "tropical" meant "tacky," at least as far as Lockett could tell from the grass shack look of the place and the cutesy drinks shaped like coconuts and pineapples. There was even a pair of pink flamingoes under a big plastic palm tree near the doors to the terrace.

So far, no one had gone out to the terrace or the pool—it was a bit muggy out in the real world—and Lockett wondered idly what new decorative disasters awaited out there. She smiled. It might not have been her kind of party, but it *was* different. And hadn't she always had a fondness for what was different?

Meanwhile the collection of wealthy young socialites who made up the guest list continued to toss back the potent punch with carefree abandon. In fact, most of the guests seemed to be thoroughly sloshed at this point. Maybe it was because they kept insisting on offering rum-laden toasts to the guest of honor.

Who was, of course, Lockett.

She was trying to be brave and get into the rather raucous spirit of the evening. She wasn't succeeding.

"You need to loosen up a little," Tish said loudly. She elbowed Lockett, sloshing her own coconut full of piña colada. "You'd better have fun while you still can. After tomorrow, it'll be too late."

"Oh, right," Lockett said weakly. *After tomorrow...*

In what was being billed as *the* nuptial event of the season, Lockett Kensington would wed Stanford Marsh, the successful, solid young executive her parents loved. Tomorrow.

"Oh, God," she whispered. "I'm supposed to get married tomorrow."

She reached for the pale peach drink and took a healthy swallow. She didn't know what it was, but it was strong enough to curl her eyelashes.

"You look really grim," her little sister Beatrice murmured from one side. "What's wrong with you?"

"Nothing."

What could be wrong? She was all set to be the perfect bride at the perfect wedding with the perfect groom. Stanford was, after all, well, *perfect*. Quite the catch, even for a member of Chicago's old aristocracy like Lockett. He had all the right attributes and credentials to be an A-1 husband.

So why was his bride-to-be so miserable?

It was exactly what she'd been asking herself for the past few days, ever since the wedding had begun to loom too close to ignore. Caught up in choosing the cake and the flowers, puttering around with china and silver choices, she'd almost forgotten she'd actually have to get married at the end of all the fun stuff.

Married. To Stanford Marsh.

She would become Lockett Kensington Marsh, elegantly groomed to preside at charity balls and sit on all the right charity boards, with a house in the country and a lakefront condo in the city. Her schedule would consist of shopping and tennis lessons, with a little time reserved for mud packs and manicures.

But she hated all of that. She always had. Besides, she had a business to run—a life to lead. She couldn't get married!

What have I done?

"What are you doing?" Beatie demanded.

"Getting married," she said resolutely. She took another swig of the potent peach drink.

"You don't have to marry that bore," her sister persisted. "There's still time to get out of it."

"I could just imagine the uproar if I tried to cancel it at this late date," she murmured dryly.

Beatie turned to her with reproving eyes. "Lockett! You never used to care about making an uproar. You used to do what you wanted. What's happened to you?"

"Maybe I grew up," she returned.

But she didn't like the truth in Beatie's words. There had been a time when she would've laughed at the idea of marrying someone as stable and respectable as Stanford Marsh. She would've said he lacked spirit. She would've said *she* craved adventure. So what had happened to that Lockett?

Was it true? Somewhere along the line, had she developed a stodgy side?

But she'd been through so many eligible suitors. It was depressing never to find anyone just right. And her parents had begun to despair that she'd ever marry. Yet remaining unmarried—letting the Kensington dynasty falter—was not even a choice in her parents' minds. She'd tried not to give in, but the pressure to wed was finally too much to hold out against. She was so tired of being a rebel, of making waves in the Kensington's well-ordered world. She was also tired of being single in a world of husbands and wives and families.

Women she'd gone to prep school with were now the proud mothers of five- and six-year-olds. And what was she? The same old Lockett Kensington.

Restless, ready to be someone new, she'd started to think that maybe getting married and starting a family nest of her own was exactly what she needed.

So she'd given in and said yes to Stanford Marsh.

But had she made the right choice? Was she doing the right thing?

"Who cares about a little uproar?" Beatie persisted.

Once upon a time Lockett had shared Beatie's opinion. Who cared whether Mother and Dad were having fits? Spoiled princess Lockett Kensington did as she pleased.

But that was before. Before a lot of things.

Now she was older and wiser, and she had begun to see the value of living a stable, well-ordered, comfortable life. A life as Mrs. Stanford Marsh.

"Stanford is everything I've ever wanted in a man," she said softly.

"Oh, puh-leez. Nobody else here may have met the first one, but I did." Beatie's smile sparkled with mischief. "I know what you like in a man. Excitement, adventure...romance! And that's nothing like our pal Stanford, the drip of the Western world."

Lockett felt a tingle of panic, like she always did when *he* was mentioned. Beatie hadn't even bothered to say his name, but Lockett knew exactly who she was talking about.

The first one, she'd called him.

Beatie's grin widened. "I remember what he looked like. After him, how could you possibly settle for Stanford?"

"After him, how could I possibly want anyone like him again?" she asked in a desperate tone. "Maybe I want Stanford because he's nothing like *Ryan*."

There it was, out in the open. His name. And it hadn't hurt that badly, had it?

"But he was exciting. He was *cool*."

"Excitement isn't everything." She knew that from painful experience. In this particular case, excitement had meant an unmitigated disaster.

"Oh, pooh. You never should've let him go." Beatrice heaved an extravagant sigh. At seventeen, she had a tendency to take herself a bit too seriously.

She also bore an extraordinary resemblance to Lockett at seventeen, which was when she'd met... Him. The *husband* who was such a mistake that no one in her social circle even knew he existed.

Her father had made sure of that.

Her hasty marriage had been such a monumental embarrassment that it was promptly blotted from the Kensington family history. Her parents never mentioned him, and neither did Lockett. Only Beatrice, who'd been nine when the whole thing had transpired, seemed inclined to dredge up memories of Lockett's dreadful first husband.

As far as Lockett was concerned, it was better not mentioning him at all.

Better to have loved and lost than never to have loved at all? Not in her book. Much, much better to have never met *him* in the first place.

"Your memory is playing tricks on you," Lockett told her sister carelessly. "He wasn't that exciting. Besides, he's long gone. I certainly don't know why you've developed this unreasonable dislike for Stanford, but you'd better get used to him. After tomorrow, he'll be your brother-in-law."

"Don't remind me."

"Beatie—"

But she was interrupted by a very inebriated guest on the other side of the party. It was Muffin Morgan, a snobby, lumpy sort of girl Lockett had known since grammar school. "Tish, you promised we'd be getting to the good part any minute," Muffin proclaimed in a loud, sloppy voice. "You said there was going to be a str—"

"Shh-hh!" commanded Tish. "It's supposed to be a surprise."

"Well, where is he? This party is a drag."

"A drag," Muffin's equally odious sister Gigi chorused. "Bring on the guys."

"Guys? What guys?" Lockett asked.

She suddenly got the terrible idea that muscle-bound men were going to start popping out of cakes or something. Is that what people did at bachelorette parties?

"Be quiet. He isn't here yet," Tish shouted above the din.

"Who?" Lockett demanded.

"Keep it down," somebody else yelled. "I thought I heard the doorbell."

"The doorbell—go see if it's him."

"The pirate? Is that him?"

"It's him!" another woman called from the direction of the hall.

"Pirate?" Lockett echoed. "What pirate?"

"Your very own pirate," Tish said with a heavy wink. "I ordered him from StripperGrams, just for you. I wanted the Scottish Stud, but he was already booked for tonight. I thought a pirate would fit my theme better, anyway. You know, like we were castaways in a tropical paradise, and in walked the Passionate Pirate. Kinky, huh?" She pushed Lockett back onto a sofa and then snaked backward through the crowd toward the double doors into the hall. "Sit down and enjoy yourself. I'll go warm up the pirate for you."

"Warm up the..." Lockett got to her feet. She was no prude, but she couldn't think of anything less appealing than sitting in Tish Bingwell's living room while a bunch of drunken socialites drooled all over some sleazy guy who was probably wearing nothing but an eye patch and an earring.

"Oh, come on," Beatie protested, catching her arm and pulling her back. "You might as well see what he looks like. Where's your spirit of adventure?"

"A s-stripper?" she sputtered. "No way."

"The stripper is here!" someone shouted. "He's fabulous."

"What a hunk. You can take it off for me any time, honey," Muffin hooted.

But Tish's strained voice rose above the rest. "I was supposed to get a pirate. What are you? A motorcycle guy? The leather look is nice and all, but where's my pirate?"

A tall, dark man dressed all in black—jeans, T-shirt, biker's jacket—strode into the center of Tish Bingwell's tropical travesty of a living room. Wearing a grim expression, he scanned the room.

"I'm looking for Lockett," he said tersely.

Of course he was. As her sister choked, Lockett stared at him in utter disbelief.

This man was no pirate. This was her ex-husband.

But it couldn't be.

She closed her eyes. This couldn't be happening. She was hallucinating, that was all.

She opened one eye.

Her stomach started to tango. She couldn't breathe. *This can't be happening.*

Under her breath, she exhaled one word. "Ryan..."

SIXTEEN and three-quarters, with more dreams than she knew what to do with, Lockett Elizabeth Kensington had the world at her feet.

Dreams. Aspirations. Ambitions. She was positively bursting with them.

Her mother had just brought up brochures for a couple of college trips, but Lockett tossed them carelessly off the end of her bed. It was summer—hot and sultry—with only a few months' freedom before she began her senior year of high school.

Mother had already told her it was time to make her college plans, now, before her senior year started. According to Marjorie Kensington, Lockett had two choices: Bryn Mawr or Vassar. Possibly she'd bend so far as to include Harvard if Lockett really pushed the point. Summer trips to visit the proper schools were already in the works.

But Lockett had no intention of attending any of those silly, stuffy, unbearable places.

She wanted freedom. She wanted to go to Paris.

Catching her hair up in a careless ponytail, Lockett smiled at her reflection in the mirror above her vanity. It was going to be tricky to make her plan work, but she was determined to see it through.

Paris. She sighed. It was going to be *fabulous*.

She excelled at artistic pursuits, but she was also very good at plain old English and math. To her mother, that translated to a few years studying art history, or perhaps some sort of design, just so she could properly decorate or serve on museum boards when she ascended to her rightful place in society.

But Lockett had dreams.

She wanted to study art—and life—and she wanted to do it in Paris.

She had every intention of convincing her parents that the best school for her was the Sorbonne. And once she was safely in Paris, she'd ditch her classes and begin to live. She'd do whatever she pleased. She'd live by her own rules and throw every last stuffy Kensington regulation out the window!

She could imagine it now—tiny cafés, crowded streets, late nights, bright lights. She'd fall in love, maybe two or three times. She'd have an affair with a painter or a sculptor—someone sexy and disreputable who lived in a tiny garret and smoked black cigarettes.

Lockett laughed out loud, hugging her daydreams close to her soul, whirling on the pale pink carpet of her luxurious bedroom.

Life was going to be spectacular. Just as soon as she got outside the dreary walls of the Kensington mansion.

But then she happened to open her bedroom window. Such a simple thing. Something she'd done a million times. And yet that one small act changed everything.

As she danced around the room, thinking about Paris and the scruffy artist she planned to make love with, she happened to idly gaze outside.

And she saw *him*.

The man was spectacular. She'd never seen anyone who looked like that working on the Kensington estate.

Stripped to the waist, glistening with sweat, he was the most gorgeous thing she'd ever seen. Soft black hair fell over his brow and into his deep, mysterious eyes. Hard, tight muscles bunched and shifted in his beautifully sculpted arms and chest. Those weren't the kind of muscles you got from playing tennis. They were hard-work-and-perspiration muscles.

Lockett's mouth went dry. She was gripping the windowsill so tightly her fingers began to cramp.

Who was he? And what was he doing down there?

When she began to breathe again, she saw, of course, that he was digging a hole for a new tree, right under her bedroom window. And if he was doing that, he must be the gardener's new assistant her father had so casually mentioned.

She licked her lips. She was having the most wicked thoughts. But one look at him and suddenly she was in the mood for a little fun.

Maybe this was a good time for some sunbathing. Not by the pool, but out on the lawn. Right under the nose of the new gardener's new assistant.

Lockett smiled widely, already deciding which bikini to wear. And just then, the hunk down below happened to wipe his dripping brow, to hazard a glance up above him.

His gaze skipped over the lawn, up the trellis, over the windowsill . . . and found Lockett.

Their eyes met.

Lockett felt the heat of his look scorch her right down to the innermost core of her being. Suddenly, Paris and the disreputable painter in the garret seemed to vanish before her very eyes.

And she knew her life would never be the same.

Chapter Two

Bachelorette Bingo

Ex-husbands do not show up at bachelorette parties pretending to be strippers, she said to herself, as if it were some sort of mantra.

She still hadn't decided if he were real or some kind of illusion. Maybe he was a figment of her peach-and-rum-soaked imagination.

Should she pinch him to be sure? Pinching *herself* seemed a heck of a lot safer.

But he was still there.

"Oh, my God," she said slowly. It was a sort of plea, a last prayer, as if appealing to a higher power might make him go away.

But he didn't go away. He turned to look at her. His face was leaner, his hair longer, his deep green eyes as beautiful and as devastating as she remembered.

It had been a long time.

"Eight years," she said out loud. It only added to the general air of incredulity about the whole thing. Eight long years. She'd thought she was safe.

She hadn't seen him in all that time. God, he looked great. But then, he always had.

Antonio Ryan. The one and only.

But what was he doing here?"

A million other questions danced in her brain. Where had he been? Where had he come from, all of a sudden?

And who had he been sleeping with all this time?

"I don't care about that," she whispered with an edge of hysteria. "That's the least of my worries at the moment."

"You know," Beatie said innocently, now that she'd recovered her voice, "I think this is the best-looking stripper I've ever seen. Don't you think so, Lockett?"

"I think I'm going to be sick."

"Oh, come on—he's not that bad." Beatie danced over and linked her arm through his. "I think he's quite a hunk, as strippers go."

Ryan, damn his hide, smiled down at her sister. He and Beatie had always gotten along like gangbusters. Meanwhile, Lockett couldn't think of a single thing to say to get herself out of this mess. Her arms hung limp at her sides as she stood there, gaping at him, shocked down to her shoes.

Ryan had always taken her breath away. Now he'd taken her vocabulary, as well.

All she could think of was, *Eight years. I haven't touched him in eight years.*

But her fingers still remembered exactly what he felt like. Skin. Muscle. Bone. So strong and so soft. Her head was spinning, but her damn fingers were feeding her the tactile memory of his sleek black hair and his hard, lean body.

Her long-parched senses drank him in. The sight of him was headier than any rum.

"Oh, my God," she said again, but it was louder and more desperate this time.

"I think Lockett is quite taken with our stripper," Tish said coyly. "So let's get stripping, shall we? Where's your music, cutie? Weren't you supposed to bring a tape recorder?"

"I'm sure we can all hum something for him," Beatie interjected. "What would you like, Mr. Stripper? How about a few bars of 'Whoomp, There It Is'?"

Still disoriented, Lockett shook her head. "This is crazy. Does *he* look like a stripper?"

"Absolutely," someone called out behind her.

"I hope so," Gigi Morgan chorused.

"Those jeans look real to me. Tight, too. How do you suppose he gets out of them?" With a gleam in her eye, Muffin moved in closer, reaching for Ryan's pants. "Do these pull apart when you yank on them, honey buns?"

Without thinking, Lockett slapped the woman's hand away. Ryan didn't appear to notice; he kept his eyes on Lockett, never wavering, as if he were waiting for her to make the first move.

Oh, sure. She was a mass of conflicting emotions. She was on the edge of hysteria. Meanwhile, the man who had caused all this uproar, the very person who was making her quiver like a bowlful of jelly, had the unmitigated gall to just stand there, watching her, acting about as affected as a block of granite.

Talk about a blast from the past. Lockett was stunned and horrified all at once.

Words seemed to pop out of her mouth without any conscious thought. "Why did you show up now?" she cried. "I'm getting married tomorrow!"

"He knows that," Beatie said at the same time. "What do you think he's doing here?"

"I don't know what he's doing here!"

"He's stripping!" Tish retorted.

"He's rescuing you," Beatie insisted.

"Rescuing me?"

"Obviously he's going to carry you off to keep you from marrying that twit," her sister said, as if it were the most natural thing on earth.

"Carry her off?" Tish asked, clearly in a state of major confusion. "Carry her off? I didn't pay for that. Is that extra?"

"I can't believe this is happening." Lockett raised a hand to her forehead. It felt hot and moist to the touch. Terrific. She was dizzy, scared to death, and now she was running a fever.

And the sweet, potent peach drink she'd gulped down began to churn in her stomach.

"Come on," Tish commanded. "Let's get this show on the road. Take it off, big boy!"

"Leave it on," Lockett said frantically. "Don't you dare take anything off!"

Ryan managed a small smile. He reached for the zipper on his jacket.

Lockett began to see fuzzy spots of light in the periphery of her vision.

Ryan as a *stripper?* He couldn't be! But what if he was? She had no idea what he did for a living, although she had always suspected he would end up doing something scandalous.

But could he be reduced to taking off his clothes to earn money?

"Ryan?" she whispered thickly. He moved closer. How odd that his face was out of focus.

The fuzzy spots grew larger, brighter. And then the pink flamingoes and the tropical blooms in Tish's living room all faded away in a pretty wash of pastel watercolors.

And everything went black.

TRUST LOCKETT to take a dive right into his arms. She always had had a melodramatic streak a mile wide.

"Get back," he said roughly. "Give her some air."

One glimpse of him, and she'd fainted dead away. Ryan clenched his jaw. So much for fond reunions.

As the noise level of the women around him rose by the minute, he shuffled Lockett into a better position, hoisting her up into his arms as he shoved his way through the crowd.

If these women would just get out of the way...

"Lockett," he muttered. "Time to wake up."

She mumbled something, but she was limp and heavy in his arms. When she woke up and figured out exactly whose arms she'd pitched herself into, she was going to be furious. Ryan smiled.

"What's happening?" someone shouted.

"Is she okay?"

"Where is the stripper going?"

"Wait—is that the doorbell? Would someone please go and get the door?"

"Forget the door—see if Lockett's okay!" a voice commanded from the other side of the pack. He thought it might be Beatie, Lockett's little sister.

"I'm sure she's fine. Just a little too much to drink," somebody yelled back. "Did anyone answer the door?"

"Would everyone please stop pushing?"

"Tish, Tish, it's another one! The Passionate Pirate is here!"

"Two strippers?"

"I like the first one better."

"Forget the stupid pirate! Let me through, will you?" Beatie said anxiously. "Ryan, is Lockett okay?"

"She'll be fine," he called back. "Just a little woozy. I'm taking her outside."

The room suddenly erupted into catcalls and squeals of delight over the strains of "Do You Think I'm Sexy?" The real stripper had obviously arrived with a fanfare.

Meanwhile, Lockett was starting to stir in his arms. Ryan maneuvered up to the terrace doors, brushing away an insistent hand massaging his back pocket. Damn women, anyway. He didn't know whether to be insulted or amused that they had mistaken him for their stripper.

Not that there was anyone in this roomful of spoiled society women he would've considered taking his clothes off for, anyway. Anyone but Lockett, of course.

Just like always, he was doing things for her. Going out on a limb for Lockett. It had once been a way of life. He'd thought he was well past that nonsense. Guess not.

Meanwhile, his ex-wife felt warm and alive in his arms as she murmured something incoherent that included his name. He knew he was going to have to find a way to set her down before he forgot why he was here and kept on carrying her.

But she felt good. Too familiar. Too right.

He suddenly remembered, with crystal clarity, carrying his bride over the threshold of their first apartment. What it felt like to be young and in love, trusting and tender, coursed through his veins.

He dropped her.

As she stumbled to her feet, still clinging to him, he managed to steer them both through the terrace doors and out into the summer air.

Better.

Lockett's eyelashes fluttered and she raised dazed eyes to his. "I hope I'm dreaming."

"You're not."

She sighed deeply. "I was afraid of that." And then she quite delicately removed her hands from his shoulders, edging away, lifting a hand to her brow. "I—I need some air."

"Right." Ryan closed the terrace doors firmly behind them as Lockett tiptoed over to the rail overlooking the pool.

The difference between the raucous scene they'd left behind and this quiet terrace was like night and day.

It wasn't just the change in temperature, as they gave up the air-conditioning for stickier, more oppressive heat. Or even the change in the sound around him, as he went from cacophony to thick silence.

No, the difference was Lockett.

There she was, silhouetted in the moonlight, her lithe body sheathed in an expensive white dress, and her soft, golden hair shining like a million bucks.

That was Lockett, all right. Even her hair reminded him of money.

He ought to be bitter. Hell, he *was* bitter. She'd run out on him, after all. Not enough bucks, the going got tough, and Lockett was out of there.

Idiotic as it was, he couldn't look at Lockett and not feel the familiar ache of desire, the familiar rush of hunger....

He was acting like a prize chump.

One minute in Lockett's presence and he'd started to get weak in the knees. He wouldn't have come here if he hadn't felt sure she was out of his system. After all, she was the one who'd betrayed him. No amount of lust could cover that up.

He let out a pent-up breath. Time to get on with this, and get away from her and the bad karma she represented in his life.

"Lockett," he called out softly. "We have to talk."

But she didn't turn. She leaned away from him, over the terrace rail, gazing down into the pool area below.

Pensive, cool, the golden girl of all his adolescent fantasies. She was beautiful.

Ryan shoved his hands into his jeans' pockets. *She's not for you, buddy.*

He strode closer. "Lockett? Did you hear me?"

She turned. Lightly, mockingly, she said, "I've always heard you. It's just that I generally chose not to listen."

Same old Lockett.

"I'm on a mission of mercy." He managed a cynical smile. "So just let me say what I came to say, and then you can listen or not, whatever you want."

"A mission of mercy?" She lifted one perfect golden eyebrow. "You? I've been imagining all sorts of reasons you showed up, but mercy wasn't among them."

He advanced on her. "Why would that be so hard to believe?"

Her eyes were wide and blue, and he caught a momentary tremble in her bottom lip. "You've never been the merciful type," she whispered.

He moved in closer, enjoying the sparks he saw in her eyes, energy he was creating. He laid a hand on the railing behind her, trapping her on one side, almost but not quite touching her.

Her eyes met his. Her lips parted slightly. He could see she was having trouble catching her breath.

Excitement. Fury. Exhilaration. He read it in her eyes, and he felt it in his gut. As if nobody else on the planet had the ability to make her so crazy, so happy, so damn mad, all in one fell swoop. And he felt exactly the same way.

He was overcome with an amazing, agonizing need to kiss her and wrap her in his arms. It had always been this way between them.

One look, one breath, and he was back on an emotional roller coaster. He muttered, "I thought maybe you'd forgotten by now."

"People don't usually forget train wrecks and nuclear explosions." Her voice was a little shaky, but he could tell Lockett was doing her best to pretend there were no flames rising between them. "So, Ryan, tell me—why are you here? I'm guessing it has something to do with my wedding. The timing makes that pretty obvious. How did you find out? About the wedding, I mean."

"It's been in all the papers."

"Not in anything I'd expect you to read."

He shrugged. "I guess my reading habits have changed since you knew me."

"I guess so."

"You looked great in the engagement pictures," he said softly, recklessly. "Just great."

Her gaze measured him, as if she weren't sure how to take a compliment. Arguments she could handle. But compliments obviously made her nervous. "And so you crashed my party to tell me you liked my photo? Why don't I believe that?''

There was a pause. Ryan dismissed her words with a curt wave of one hand. Abruptly he said, "I'm not going to let you marry that guy."

Lockett shook her head and tossed her hair back over her shoulders. Without a word, she pushed away from him, gliding down the stairs toward the pool with her filmy white dress wafting behind her.

"Still running away, Lockett? Is that the best defense you can come up with?"

She didn't answer. He cursed himself for charging in and screwing things up before he'd even gotten started. Why did being around her seem to put his brain on hold?

He ambled down the steps behind her, purposely casual. "Lockett," he tried. "Just listen for a few seconds, okay? We can get this over with."

She stared down at the pool, resolutely not looking at him. "I think you should go away."

Was that fear he heard in her voice? Lockett, afraid of him? "I can't."

"Yes, you can." She smiled, with her patented Lady of the Manor charm. "You put one foot in front of the other, just like you did when you walked in here. Before you know it, you're gone. It's easy."

"That's your strategy, not mine."

She whirled. "I don't know what you're doing here, and I don't care. Showing up the day before my wedding..." She shook her head in disbelief. "Your arrogance still has the power to amaze me. You just waltz in here and tell me who I am not allowed to marry, and I'm supposed to say, 'Oh, okay. Whatever you want, Ryan.' Well, I don't do what I'm told anymore. I do what *I* want." She shook her head again. "I can't talk to you. I *won't* talk to you."

Her hands swung up between them, as if she had plans to hold him off. She backed up a step closer to the pool, the cool blue water, shimmering in the summer moonlight.

"Lockett—" He tried, but she wasn't listening.

"Don't you dare talk to me," she said in a warning tone. "Our marriage was over a long time ago, and you have no right to barge in here and embarrass me in front of my friends."

"Embarrass you?" He raised a dark eyebrow. "Seems to me like you should've already been about as embarrassed as it gets, what with that bunch of rich drunks drooling over a stripper."

"There's nothing wrong with—"

"Enough, Lockett. You're not fooling anyone. Those aren't your friends, and we both know it. My guess is those are the snobs Elliot and Marjorie picked out for you to pal around with."

"My parents have nothing to do with—"

He knew his bluntness was not destined to win Lockett over to his side. But he couldn't seem to dredge up any persuasive technique to help him make this palatable. The tension was simply too thick between them. Anything either of them said, no matter how innocent, raised the other's defenses.

"Your father's fingerprints are all over this," he said angrily. "He's still doing his best to run your life into the ground and you're letting him."

Lockett sucked in a sharp breath. "How dare you?"

"I dare a lot of things."

"You don't know anything about me," she argued. "I'm not the naive little girl you married eight years ago. I have a life. I run a business of my own! My father does not make my choices for me."

"You didn't choose that guy." He clenched his jaw. "I know you better than that. Daddy chose him for you."

"Don't be absurd."

She tried to push past him, but he caught her. "Lockett, this is *their* life they're leading, not yours."

"There is nothing wrong with my life," she said stubbornly.

"Except that it doesn't include any of the things I know are important to you."

"How would you know what's important to me?" She looked up. There was anger in her eyes, but also a hint of doubt, and he knew he'd slightly cracked the façade of perfection. It was a start.

"You're too good for this life," he insisted. "You're too smart and honest to end up just another superficial rich girl. Excitement, challenges—love," he told her. "Those meant something to you once."

"Not you, too?" she cried. "Why does everybody think I need *excitement* all of a sudden? I'm doing just fine being boring and safe, thank you."

"You were never fine being boring."

"So I've changed."

"No," he said flatly. "You're just lying to yourself."

"Don't talk to me about lies." There was definite fire in her eyes now. "You were the one with all the secrets. You were the one telling lies."

"Lockett," he warned.

"No," she said again. Lockett had never held her own in an argument with him like this. He was finding out exactly how much she'd changed. And he didn't like it. "Go away. Leave me alone, you, you... *snake.*"

Before he had a chance to think about the folly of his action, Ryan grabbed her, pulling her closer. He hated losing control, but she made him so damn mad. "Still the spoiled little princess, aren't you? All I get is insults, when I came here to rescue you."

"Nobody asked you," she snapped. "And I don't need to be rescued. I'm getting married tomorrow, and I'm going to live happily ever after. Without you. So you can give up on the mission right now."

But her skin was warm and soft under his fingers. Her blue eyes sparkled with life and everything that made Lockett so damn appealing. He whispered, "I can't seem to help myself."

And then he kissed her.

Chapter Three

Midnight Madness

She had forgotten what it felt like. Desperate passion, Romeo and Juliet, hot summer nights... It all came back amazingly quickly.

As Ryan made some possessive little noise and pulled her closer, nipping hungrily at her lips, delving inside, branding her once more with the heat and the ferocity of his hard mouth, Lockett's body leapt to life. She tingled. She felt little flickers of flame lick at her toes.

She always had been crazy about his mouth. The things he could do...

But some scrap of sense remained, even under this incredible assault on her defenses. When he'd first showed up, she was confused, dazed, maybe even a little dazzled. Then, after he'd proceeded to talk down to her and order her around, she'd been furious. Now she was flat out enraged.

And she had enough anger inside her, to get out of this mess before resisting became impossible.

"What are you doing?" Gasping for breath, Lockett pushed him away. "What the hell do you think you're doing?"

"Shutting you up," he said softly. "The only way I know how."

The nerve of the man! She had the urge to knock him into the pool, but she resisted. Instead she slapped him, hard, with a satisfying crack that echoed on the stone terrace.

As the imprint of her hand bloomed on his cheek, she kept her chin high.

Deadpan, he offered, "Thanks, Lockett. As usual, you really know how to tell me exactly what you're feeling."

"You deserved it."

"Right. I'm trying to pull your pretty little butt out of trouble, and I deserve to be slapped."

Under her breath, she muttered, "If you ask me, you always deserve to be slapped."

She still wasn't sure she even believed he was here. But his lips hadn't felt like any figment of her imagination.

"Oh, this is so absurd," she said suddenly, charging in, not bothering to think before she spoke. It was so unlike her to lose her cool this way—years of breeding were going right out the window—and she didn't even care. "It's ridiculous *and* insulting. You barge in here and pretend to be a stripper, practically giving me a heart attack, and then you have the gall to *kiss* me. Are you demented? Are you insane? Or is this some kind of bullying tactic? Is that it? Do you honestly think you can show up out of the blue and kiss me and I'll be so hypnotized, I'll do whatever you want?"

She knew she sounded vaguely hysterical, and she didn't care. If she'd thought it would help, she would've wiped the damn kiss off her lips. But the taste of Ryan would still be there, and they both knew it.

"I'm not trying to bully you or hypnotize you." He glared at her from beneath dark brows. "I came here for your own good. Somebody had to save you from making the biggest mistake of your life."

"No, Ryan. You've forgotten. I already made the biggest mistake of my life."

"Do you ever listen to anything I say?"

"Why should I?"

"Because this is important, Lockett. I can't let you do this."

"You said that before," she told him in an ominous tone. "You won't *let me,* you said. Since when do you let me do anything?"

"You can't marry that jerk."

"I already married one jerk," she reminded him. "And it didn't kill me."

"No pain, no regrets, no nothing. Is that it?" His eyes were a dark, moody green in the shadowy light of the pool. "You just wipe our marriage off the map, and it never existed?"

He could play his wounded act all night, and she wasn't going to give an inch. She was furious with him. In the old days she would've kept her mouth shut and let her grievances pile up. Well, not anymore. Now she was letting him have it with both barrels, and she was really proud of herself.

Ha! Let him take a few rounds of this and see who he thought he could run roughshod over.

Trying to stay relatively calm, she told him, "I never said it didn't exist. Believe me, I've got the scars to prove it."

"If you learned your lesson, then what are you doing jumping into marriage with that stooge you call a fiancé?"

The way he phrased things had always really raked her nerves. Okay, so she knew she had her own reservations about Stanford. But that didn't give Ryan the right to waltz back into her life at the eleventh hour and start issuing sermons from the mount.

"There's nothing wrong with Stanford," she said hotly. "You're just jealous. I'm marrying someone successful and dependable and truly honorable. In other words, all the things you're not and never could be."

Very old weapons. But she could tell from the harsh line of his jaw that she had hit her target.

Ryan's tone was very bitter, very dark, when he said, "It takes more than a bank account to make a good husband, Lockett. I thought you would've figured that out by now. But you never could see what was right in front of your face, could you?"

She ignored the insult, preferring to launch one of her own. "How in the world would you know what it takes to make a good husband?"

And then it hit her. She had no idea what he'd been doing the last eight years. For all she knew, he'd found another wife within a few weeks of her departure.

Lockett shot him a quick glance. "You're not married again, are you?"

He didn't answer for a long moment, just watched her steadily. "No," he said eventually. "Once was enough for me."

Oh, God. That was actually relief she felt. Fool that she was, she was relieved down to her bones to hear he hadn't remarried.

What did she care? Ryan was nothing to her. She was getting married in the morning. *He's nothing to me,* she told herself fiercely.

But he was.

He was standing there, staring her in the face, big as life. A reminder of what once was, if nothing more.

"What do you want?" she asked wearily. "Why are you torturing both of us like this?"

"Lockett, this isn't fun and games, okay? This is serious. I've stumbled across something. Something that could change everything."

"Uh-huh," she said dubiously.

"You have to get out of it before it goes any further. I'm offering my help to get you clear of the situation. Not with me," he said quickly, shoving a hand through his hair. "We both know that would never work. But I have connections."

Lockett was well aware of his connections. Funny how the very idea still hurt so much. "Your uncle Max?" she inquired. "Is that what you mean by connections?"

"He can be very useful."

"He's a gangster, Ryan," she said more sharply. "Good grief! I remember, if you don't, what dangerous games your uncle Max played. If he's doing you favors, you owe him back. I remember how that works. I remember sitting home worrying about you while you went running off doing some kind of payback for Uncle Max. Your duty, you said. He's family. Just a little favor. Only you'd be gone for weeks at a time and I didn't know whether you'd come back dead or alive, or whether you'd come back at all!"

"You never were rational on that subject."

"Rational? My husband was hobnobbing with gangsters and you expect me to be rational?" She had never felt less rational in her life. Scared to death, furious, betrayed—those were the emotions Ryan and his "connections" evoked for her.

"Don't overdo the drama, Lockett," he said with disgust.

"But drama is your life," she flung. The adventure and excitement that threaded through his life had always been his biggest attraction and his weakness. "And now? What do you do now? Did favors for Uncle Max escalate into a career, Ryan?"

"No." He shrugged. "I have nothing to do with Max or the Fiorin family. All that is well in the past."

Was that relief she felt? Okay, so she had a vestige of worry left over from the past, worry that he was living a dangerous life. It didn't mean anything.

"So what do you do?" She chewed her lip as she watched him. "Way back when, you had plans to go to law school. Did you? Are you a lawyer now?"

"No." He turned away.

"Then what?" she persisted. She found herself incredibly curious about everything that had happened to him since they'd parted. "What do you do for a living, Ryan?"

He made an impatient gesture with one hand. "You wouldn't believe me if I told you."

That didn't sound promising. Maybe he really was a stripper. "Try me," she ventured.

"Look, this isn't really important, okay? I need to tell you what I came to say." He took a deep breath, and then he edged around to face her. His face was cast in dark, severe lines. "You're in big trouble. Your father is in trouble. What I've discovered makes me believe he engineered this wedding as a last-gasp effort to save himself. But it isn't going to work."

"What are you talking about?" Wrestling away from his hands, Lockett was astonished. "My father's in trouble and he's engineering my wedding? How would you, of all people, be in a position to know that?"

Ryan sighed. "Connections, remember? I know you don't want to hear it, but it's true."

"So Uncle Max provides information now, as well as extortion and graft?"

"It's the truth," he said quietly.

"You wouldn't know the truth if it popped up and pinched you on the butt like Muffin Morgan."

He raised an eyebrow. "Who's Muffin Morgan?"

"That lumpy woman who was so enamored of your jeans in there... Oh, never mind!" Impatient, feeling more than a bit steamed, she clamped down on the impulse to stamp her foot. "Well?"

"Well, what?"

"Get on with it, will you? What's this important information Uncle Max provided that you're just dying to share? You know, whatever it is that puts me and my father in such dire straits?"

"Your wedding."

"I know this is about my wedding," she stormed. "What about it?"

Flat out, Ryan announced, "Your father is selling you to the highest bidder."

Lockett almost laughed. "You're overlooking the small fact that *I* chose to accept Stanford's proposal. Me, not my father." She crossed her arms over her chest. "You can do better than that, Ryan."

He caught her elbow, turning her to face him. And then he reached out a hand to smooth her hair back into place where she had tousled it. She had to concentrate very hard not to feel the brush of his fingers near her cheek, not to turn into putty under his touch.

Dropping his voice, acting the role of an earnest, sincere pal, he said, "Your father's in trouble, Lockett. Max wouldn't tell me much, but I know that your father and fiancé are up to their necks in it."

Too bad she wasn't buying any of it. She swatted his hands away from her arm and her hair. "My father is happy I'm marrying someone he likes, someone who can take care of me. That's it as far as collusion goes."

"Don't do it again, Lockett."

"Do what? Marry someone who's only after my money?" Mockingly she announced, "I already did that, thanks. This time I'm going for someone whose motives are aboveboard, someone with money of his own who doesn't need mine."

Muttering an oath, Ryan swung away from her. "No matter what, you never will believe me, will you? When it comes to my word against dear old Dad's, you'll pick his every time."

"I'm not going to discuss this," she said, skirting around him, heading for the stairs.

But he blocked her path. "Are you afraid to hear that your father is still a liar and a cheat, just like he always was? I know he told you all kinds of lies to get you away from me the first time, and I also know his business practices are anything but aboveboard. I haven't had time to really get the goods on him yet—"

"How could you possibly know any of that?" she demanded.

Ryan's voice dropped into a cool, dangerous zone. "It's easy to get information when you want it. And I wanted it on your father." He smiled, so coldly that Lockett felt chilled just looking at him. "Let's just say I make it my business to keep track of my old enemies."

"Your enemy?" she echoed. This sounded like a bad old movie. "Oh, I get it. Because of what happened between you and me, you cast my father in the role of your enemy. And now you've decided to make up a bunch of malarkey to settle this ancient score. You and your family," she said meaningfully, "never did play fair."

"My family and I play fairer than you and yours."

His green eyes held her. If she hadn't known better, she would've sworn that was honesty shining there. *No way.* Ryan didn't have an honest bone in his body.

"I don't know what he told you to get you to leave me, but it wasn't true," he said tersely. "Your father is a liar, Lockett. He always has been."

Lockett shook her head slowly. "That this still matters to you after so long is what really stuns me. Why, Ryan? Why now?"

A long pause hung between them.

Roughly, Ryan murmured, "I admit there's a score to settle. It matters to me that you finally see what was true and what wasn't. But that's not all." He edged away, staring into the water, giving her the full benefit of his breathtaking profile. "Your father brought it back up, Lockett. Him, not me. I was minding my own business, getting along with my life. *He* was the one who dealt me into this game."

"It's not a game," Lockett insisted.

"He's sold you off to Stanford Marsh, like some kind of high-class bait for a business merger. And yet you still refuse to see him for what he is."

She wouldn't listen. She had enough problems with Stanford and this wedding herself, without adding Ryan's insane charges to the mix. There was no way to get out of it, even if she'd wanted to. Things had gone too far. So it made no sense to listen to any of this craziness.

Besides, she was sure Ryan was just pulling some new scam, and that was all. He always had tried to blame her father for his own inadequacies. Once upon a time, she had bought his line.

Even as she mulled it over and made it work in the framework of her own mind, she couldn't get away from one very upsetting fact: Ryan thought so little of her that he didn't believe another man could love her and want her for herself. No, it all had to be part of a big plot, some dirty, low-down machinations from her father.

Carefully, trying not to show how much it hurt, she said, "Just because you never loved me doesn't mean Stanford feels the same way."

There was a long pause. "Who said I never loved you?"

She really didn't want to hear this. She couldn't stand hearing this.

"I really want you to go away now," she whispered. "If you could just humor me in this, I would greatly appreciate it."

"Not quite yet, Lockett. I have one more thing to tell you, one last bit of home truth."

He leaned in closer. His breath puffed hot and soft against her cheek, and she could smell the dark, worn leather of his jacket. Lockett closed her eyes, but it didn't make any of it go away.

"I just thought you should know. Good old Dad Kensington is so insecure about your upcoming nuptials that he hired someone to keep me away from you until after it's all over. You'd think eight years of us being apart would be enough for him to feel secure.

Funny thing is, I had no intention of coming anywhere near you until I ran into his henchmen. I don't like being ordered around."

She swallowed past a dry throat. What was he saying? His words were lost in the sensation of standing way too close and remembering way too much.

"Once his men came out and told me to stay away from you, I decided I ought to figure out why." His voice grew a shade huskier, stroking her frayed nerves. "It just didn't make sense he'd get nervous after all this time. So I asked myself, why is your father so afraid you won't go through with it that he resorts to a crazy tactic like that? Pretty odd, isn't it? Figure it out for yourself, Lockett. Your dad is awfully hot to marry you off to Stanford Marsh. But why?"

"Because he loves me," she whispered. "He wants the best for me, and he knows that's Stanford. You interfered in the past. Maybe he was afraid you would again. It's not so odd."

"After eight years? Oh, yes, it is."

And damn the man—he was right. It was odd. It was downright bizarre. Why would her father disturb a hornet's nest after all these years? She really didn't want to think about this.

Ryan stepped back, releasing her. "Think about it, Lockett. Think about who always comes to your rescue when you need it the most."

And then he was gone.

Lockett opened her eyes. She was alone on the terrace, staring into the cool, clear blue water of the Bingwell pool.

Think about who always comes to your rescue when you need it the most.

It wasn't hard. Standing there, by the side of a swimming pool, it wasn't hard at all. . . .

HER SEVENTEENTH BIRTHDAY. A lavish pool party at the Kensington estate. No parents around.

Although none of them were old enough to drink legally, there was plenty of liquid refreshment. The pool house had a fully stocked bar, and partygoers just fixed themselves whatever they wanted.

Several of the boys had imbibed a bit too much before they'd gotten to the party, but Lockett hadn't really paid much attention. They were loud and obnoxious, but that was nothing new—she'd grown to expect that kind of behavior from the wealthy, spoiled kids in her crowd. Besides, what did she care what they did?

No, she was worried about her new bikini, a pale cocoa suede number with a few beads and some fringe in the more obvious places. It was very racy, but she was seventeen.

Besides, she was hoping the gardener's assistant, that dark, handsome boy she'd spotted a few weeks ago, would amble by the pool. She knew he was cutting the grass today, and that ought to bring him within range sooner or later. Maybe he would take one look at her in her bikini and be as smitten as she was.

She'd seen him again yesterday, half-naked, gleaming with sweat, mopping his brow with a discarded T-shirt after he'd slashed a bunch of bushes into shape.

He was *hot*. And so was Lockett, just thinking about the picture he made. The boy's she dated were just that—kids. But he was a man.

So far he hadn't given her the time of day, even if she was a Kensington, and him just a servant.

Still, there was a look in his eye that told her he wasn't immune. She knew she was playing with fire; she knew she shouldn't be toying with the hired help, but still . . . She was hoping he'd see her in this new bikini.

And then things started to get out of hand. A few of the boys were playing some kind of drinking game, and they talked the girls into it, too. They seemed to get louder and more out of control, with a lot of sexual innuendo and hysterical laughter added to the mix.

Suddenly a girl Lockett barely knew was tottering on the end of the diving board, smiling and laughing drunkenly as she peeled off her suit. She dove in, but the boys chased after her quickly, three or four of them, with a whole lot of groping and giggling going on under the water.

Somebody was shrieking, lots of people were shedding their swimsuits, somebody else was pouring down a whole bottle of vodka while people cheered him on, and one couple started to show every intention of making love in the shallow end of the pool with another cadre of people cheering *them* on.

Lockett began to get very scared. It was the middle of the afternoon at her parents' house—she hadn't expected an orgy.

"Stop it!" she tried. But no one was paying any attention.

A boy named Skip grinned at her, lunging as if he planned to tear off her bikini top, but she pushed him backward into the pool, out of range.

She was so frightened and helpless. But it didn't stop. Someone else came at her and tried to kiss her, breathing liquor-soaked breath on her, and she elbowed him hard in the gut.

He called her a few names, but he left her alone.

What could she do? She couldn't call the police—her father would be embarrassed and incensed that she'd publicly humiliated his household. There were only a few servants around, and none of them was going to take on a whole poolful of drunk kids. Except . . .

The assistant gardener.

He looked like he could whip most of the juvenile jerks in the pool with one hand tied behind his back. Lockett raced to the stone wall surrounding the pool, hoisting herself up far enough to see over it.

He was a hundred yards away, roaring around on the back of the riding lawn mower. "Hey!" she shouted, waving her arms. "Over here! I need your help!"

She knew he couldn't hear her, but somehow their eyes made contact. She waved again, more frantic this time.

It seemed like it took him forever, but he switched off the mower and ambled over her way, looking self-conscious and wary.

And then he was there, on the other side of the wall, waiting.

His hair was in his eyes again, although he wiped at it with the back of one hand, and she could see the perspiration beaded on his forehead. He was tanned and fit, beautifully muscled. Even wearing a ratty old T-shirt and a pair of disreputable gym shorts, he looked fabulous.

Lockett's mouth went dry.

"I need your help," she mumbled. "My party—it's gotten crazy." She could hear the screams and splashes behind her, still rising in volume. "Please? Can you help?"

Without further ado, he swung himself over the wall, landing neatly beside her. But he still hadn't said a word.

And then, as easily as that, he fixed it. With a grim look in his eye, he quietly locked the pool house and cleaned all the booze off the patio. And then he started to drain the pool.

It was a lot tougher for people to misbehave without anything to drink or any place to play. A few of the jerks tried to fight with him, but he quelled that pretty quick, too. They were boys; he was a man. It was a simple as that. And Lockett's eyes grew wider, shinier, mistier.

He was her hero.

He was the most gorgeous, most dangerous, most manly thing she'd ever seen. How could she not be swept off her feet?

And when order had been restored and all the rowdy guests shipped out, she leaned up on tiptoe to kiss his cheek, to offer her thanks. Her hero blushed.

His gaze swept over her provocative little bikini, and she knew it had achieved the desired effect. He raised a hand, reaching out to finger a bead on her top, very gently, barely pushing it back and forth.

"Thank you," she said again. "For rescuing me."

"All in a day's work," he murmured. But his gaze was hot and steady, and she knew this was only the beginning between them. . . .

How LONG had she been standing there, staring at the pool, remembering times long gone?

"Ryan?" she called out. But he had already left.

She still felt like the girl at the pool, waiting for Prince Charming to come and slay her dragons. But she was older now, and wiser. Wasn't she?

But if she was so much wiser, what was she doing letting him walk away? There was so much unfinished business between them.

She was getting married tomorrow. No matter what Ryan said, no matter what he did to her, she *was* getting married tomorrow. And this might be her last chance to talk to him, to stop fighting long enough to put the past and the ashes of their marriage to rest.

"Ryan?" she called again.

Before she had a chance to change her mind, she tore off around the house to where her car was parked. Her purse was back inside the Bingwell living room, but she had an extra ignition key hidden under the mat. If she hurried, she might be able to catch him before he found his way out of the winding streets in this high-priced subdivision. After all, she knew this place better than he did, and there was only one way out.

He would have to get back to the main gates, and she could beat him there. She was sure of it.

Lockett jumped into her Porsche and raced to the gates, just in time to see a man on a sleek red motorcycle zoom out onto the highway. She was no more than a few hundred yards behind him, and she began to feel the rising excitement of the chase.

The pavement was black and shiny in the humid summer night; her lights cast an eerie glow into the darkness. Ryan was well ahead, traveling recklessly, crisscrossing small shaded streets and unfamiliar highways as he headed steadily south toward the city.

Of course, he had the advantage of knowing where he was headed, and she could only follow, but still . . . She had the sense that he was toying with her, purposely pushing her to go faster than she was comfortable with, letting her get only so close before he would open up the distance between them again.

Where was he going?

When they'd split up, when she'd left him to return to her parents' house, she really hadn't known where he would go or how he would live. She hadn't let herself think about it. She'd known somehow that he would not stay in their apartment, that he would leave New York where they had set up camp in their mad dash to be away from her parents in Illinois, away from the hated school in Maine.

But she had not considered, not for one moment, that he would end up back in Chicago, only a stone's throw from her door.

Yet he drove his bike with a sure hand and a good deal of speed, as if he knew exactly where he was headed. Home.

The lush northern suburbs eventually gave way to the pitted streets of the city. She had no idea where they were, only that they were cutting across town, through neighborhoods where she felt sure her Porsche stood out like a sore thumb. She knew the city fairly well, but only parts of it—the Gold Coast, where she shopped and played; Clybourn Street, where she owned a small boutique; even the Loop, where the Kensington Building sat not far from the Board of Trade.

But she had no idea where she was at this moment. Just following Ryan into the bowels of hell. Well, not quite that bad, but some of these areas were pretty scuzzy. Ahead of her, Ryan turned onto a bigger street. The houses and businesses were older now, with an occasional turret or tower poking into the night sky. And she thought she could smell bread, as if there was a bakery close by.

Ryan had led her to the old neighborhood where he'd grown up. She was sure of it. But there was no time to get her bearings.

He had disappeared. He had been a few cars ahead of her, well within sight, when he suddenly wasn't there anymore. Her heart beat faster. Lockett slowed considerably, peering into the murky darkness. Where had he disappeared to?

And then she caught a flash of red off to one side. The motorcycle. Relief and renewed fear, anticipation, fueled her onward. Trust Ryan to be back in her life for five minutes and have her on pins and needles already. Whatever else she felt about him, he always provided excitement.

She slipped down the side street, around the back of the small shop on the corner where she thought she'd seen that glimpse of shiny red metal.

It was a perfectly ordinary building, two-story, with a small square of grass and a garage off the driveway in back. There was a set of stairs stuck onto the back of the small structure, and a door at the top of the stairs, as if someone lived up there, over the store. The door slammed shut just as she pulled into the driveway. The sound echoed into the darkness.

Her pulse pounding, Lockett hesitated. Could Ryan possibly live up there? Or maybe he was just staying up there while he was in town to see her. But why?

And what if this wasn't Ryan? What if she'd followed some maniac by mistake when Ryan disappeared?

Cautiously she got out of the Porsche and peeked in the window to the garage. His motorcycle, with its snazzy red lines, was easy to identify.

She swallowed, trying to calm down. But it was impossible. He was definitely here. Now if only she had enough guts to walk right up to his lair and knock on the door.

Her heart hammered against her ribs as she slowly mounted the wooden steps one a time. She took a deep breath and raised a hand to knock.

But before her knuckles even touched the wood, the door swung open.

"What took you so long?" he asked. And he pulled her into his arms.

Chapter Four

Intoxicating Intimacy

The scent of flowers was overpowering. Carnations, maybe, and lilies, with a heady undercurrent of roses.

Lockett didn't stop to wonder why—there was no time, not when Ryan's arms were fast around her, when his mouth nibbled at her neck. His body was hot and strong, and she melted into him, tipping back her head, letting his lips wander where they would.

She couldn't breathe, couldn't move, couldn't do anything but just *feel*. He felt wonderful in her arms. *She* felt exultant, alive, strangely happy—just to be held this way.

The room was steamy, and maybe that's why the aroma of flowers was so intense, as if they were in a hothouse. It really didn't matter. It only contributed to the otherworldliness of this whole thing, to the feeling that she'd been swept off her feet, pitched headlong into some kind of enchantment.

Ryan didn't say a word. His mouth was otherwise occupied. Keeping the heavy, searching kiss constant, he pulled her into the room, one step at a time, half carrying and half dragging her. He stumbled as he backed up, toppling both of them over onto a sofa. Lockett couldn't see it or anything else in the pitch-black room, but she could feel the soft leather cushions underneath her.

The only light was a single shaft of moonlight from some open window, enough to make the shadows seem more oppressive and the darkness more forbidding by comparison.

"Where are we?" she whispered.

"Hush." He nipped at her mouth and her chin, as if he wanted to taste all of her right now.

He framed her face in his strong hands, stared at her for a long moment, and then covered her mouth with his. Warm, potent, intoxicating, his kiss deepened, sending Lockett down even further, way over her head.

All that existed were his clever hands, stroking her face, pressing her closer at the small of her back, and his devastating mouth, delving deeper, demanding more of her soul. She was swamped with memories, and yet it all felt fresh and new.

He knew how to push her buttons, all right. There never had been anybody who captivated her senses like Ryan. He was so good at it, and it was so tempting to lie back in his arms and let him do his magic.

Lockett raised herself a little, trying to collect herself enough to resist. She hadn't come here for this.

But Ryan angled around her, sliding warm, wet kisses over the line of her chin, down the slope of her neck. When he cradled her against the hard, lean length of his body, when his fingers barely grazed the tip of her breast through the gauzy fabric of her dress . . .

She couldn't help it.

Her heart beat faster. Every nerve ending pulsed and throbbed. It was so damn hot in the room, so heavy, so hard to breathe.

She tried to take a deep breath, to find some air, but Ryan kissed her again, and she was greedy. It had been so long. Too long to live on memories. Her arms twisted around his neck, urging him closer as she slid her fingers through his sleek, dark hair.

His hair was longer than she remembered, and it spilled over her hands, as black and soft as the darkness between them. It was so lush, it made her crazy, made her feel like she'd die right then and there if she couldn't fill her hands with the rest of him.

This was so unlike her, and yet she couldn't deny the emotions rocketing through her system. At some fundamental level she wanted to be this new, impulsive person, this wanton, wayward Lockett who took what she needed and damned the consequences.

Was that new? Or old? Had this single-minded, passion-driven recklessness been hiding inside her all this time?

But it didn't matter. What mattered was *now*, being here with Ryan.

Last chance for excitement. Last chance for romance....

Above her in the darkness, Ryan leaned down to cover her mouth with his in a swift, hungry kiss, and then he pulled back, just slightly, perhaps to catch his breath, or to find a better angle.

Lockett reached for him, trying to draw him back down to her. But she pulled too hard, upsetting their fragile balance on the sofa, and they tipped over onto the hardwood floor.

She hit the floor with a jolt.

It was like a wake-up call.

And it was enough to restore at least a little of her sanity.

"I... We..." she mumbled, scrambling away from him, pulling her clothes together.

"What?" He reached for her, but she eluded his grasp, unwilling to risk being touched. She huddled over against the wall, with the coffee table splitting the murky distance between them. "Lockett? What is it?"

"We can't," she managed. "I mean, *I* can't. Do this, I mean. With you."

A long beat of silence separated them.

"Why not?" he asked finally.

Her eyes began to adjust to the darkness, and she could see that his own gaze was dark and hooded. When he spoke, his voice sounded smoky, a shade rough.

"Why not, Lockett?" he asked. "What are we really risking? It's not like I don't already know every trick of your body, and you don't already know mine just as well. After all, this isn't anything we haven't done a million times."

A million times. Oh, God. He was right. So many times. So much heat generated between the two of them. And so much joy.

Lockett lifted her gaze to meet his. She remembered every single time. And obviously, so did he.

SHE WAS A PRINCESS. He was just a punk.

He wasn't good enough for her, not by a long shot. He knew it, and he knew she did, too, and the knowledge of just how wrong all this was ate away at him every time they were together. But it didn't keep him away.

He kept coming back for more, as long as his good fortune lasted, as long as Lockett Kensington was foolish enough to keep wanting him.

Oh, sure, he had pretentions. He planned to be somebody. Someday. But right now, she was Lockett Kensington. And he was nobody, just a kid from a so-so neighborhood with a bad family reputation.

The only thing he had was Lockett. And his dreams.

He was twenty-one, and old enough to realize that things never quite worked out the way you wanted. But he was trying to forget that, to pretend that what he had with Lockett, what he wanted from his wife, wouldn't all turn to ashes. He was trying hard.

It was only a lucky break he'd gotten the job at the Kensington estate. They'd had somebody else in mind who'd fallen through at the last minute.

Ryan was already working two other jobs—caddying full-time at a posh golf course and shelving books at the law library at the University of Chicago during odd hours. The head gardener wasn't sure he could handle another position. He was also a part-time student during the year, with his summers spent trying to put together enough cash to make it back for one more semester.

But the Kensington head gardener had a son studying pre-law, and he'd thought Ryan's aspirations were worthy of support. And so he'd hired Ryan.

Pre-law. What a joke. His uncle thought that was pretty funny. Antonio Ryan, son of Uncle Max's top lieutenant, raised at the knee of one of Chicago's shadiest men, and he wanted to be a lawyer. Max said maybe Ryan would end up *consiglière* to the Fiorin family, but he had no intention of being a mob lawyer.

He hadn't told Uncle Max, of course. He owed the old man a lot, and he didn't want to break it to him. Not yet. After both his parents had died, there'd been nobody else to take him in, but Max did. He wasn't even related, and he'd taken Ryan in, just like family. Yeah, Ryan owed the old man.

This lawyer business had taken the Fiorins by surprise. They'd all assumed he would grow up and become a soldier in the family business, like his father before him. But Ryan had other ideas. He was smart and he was ambitious, and he didn't intend to end up like his dad, in the wrong place at the wrong time, dead before he was forty.

So here he was, with an expensive, time-consuming girlfriend who came from a totally different world.

She hadn't told anyone she was dating a lowly gardener. He knew that. He understood that. Hell, in her position, he wouldn't have told anyone, either.

But the secrecy didn't stop them from being together as much as possible. In fact, it only enhanced things.

At first they were cautious. Every night she'd park her little red MG under cover of a tree around the back of the golf course where he caddied from noon to eight. Ryan would sneak out and off they'd go. Their "dates" never consisted of much—he couldn't afford to take her anywhere interesting, and he refused to even consider her footing the bills.

They mostly went back to his tiny, stuffy apartment in the city, far from the fancy suburb where Lockett lived, to the only place where they could be completely alone.

And they made love. He had restrained himself as much as he could, realizing she was not like the other girls he knew. But Lockett was so eager, so incredibly ready, there was no way Ryan could hold out.

The first time he took her to his place, they made love. And then they did it again and again, with a sense of urgency. He made love to her with a rush of passion and power, and he lost what was left of his heart.

Lithe, young, strong, beautiful—Lockett wrapped herself around his heart so tightly neither one could breathe. He just couldn't get enough. When they began, she was inexperienced; he was very experienced. It didn't matter. With her, it was all new.

She called him Tony. No one had ever called him that, except maybe his mother when he was very young. It was special. It was magic. For the rest of the world, he was Ryan, the punk with a chip on his shoulder. For Lockett, he was Tony, someone who could pretend to be newly minted, untouched, in love.

Their lovemaking was like nothing he'd ever experienced. Was he so starved for affection that loving Lockett became an obsession? Was he so conscious of his own lack of class that he was trying to absorb hers?

Ryan didn't know why. He just knew that he had to be with her.

If that meant helping her sneak out of her parents' house at all hours, jeopardizing the job he so badly needed . . . well, so be it.

Until her father found out.

He didn't know what Old Man Kensington said to her, but he could imagine. *A servant . . . So far beneath you, there's no rung on the ladder that low.*

It wasn't anything he hadn't already told himself. He was fired, summarily, by the head gardener. No reason given. But he knew.

He hadn't been back at his apartment five minutes when Lockett came running in.

"My father is furious," she cried. "I knew he wouldn't approve, but I didn't think he would go through the roof. I've never seen him like this."

"Who cares what your father thinks?" At that desperate moment, faced with the idea of losing her, Ryan was willing to toss away everything that had ever mattered to him. "Come away with me—we can get married...."

But she wouldn't, couldn't, run away with him. She hadn't been brought up like that.

Nonetheless, she wouldn't stop seeing him, either.

Until suddenly, without warning, Lockett disappeared. Her MG wasn't there when he left the golf course. No one answered the private phone in her room.

He could've assumed that she'd grown tired of him, or that she'd finally realized how wrong their love was. But he didn't think that—not for a minute.

Deep in his heart, Ryan knew what had happened. Her father had found out that they were still seeing each other, and he had sent her away.

Elliot Farnham Kensington III was a man of great influence and power. If he said his daughter was to be walled up behind the walls of some school, there wasn't anyone to stop him.

No one but Ryan.

He vowed, then and there, that he would find her, that he would rescue her. He had never felt such powerful emotions the way he did with Lockett—respected, heroic, clean and good. He needed her back, and he knew she needed him, too.

And once he found her, he would never let her go.

RYAN ROSE from the floor, leaving Lockett behind in the dark living room as he strode into the kitchen. He pulled a beer out of the refrigerator, masking his real reason for retreat. He wasn't even thirsty; he just needed to put some distance between him and his infuriating ex-wife.

"Ryan," she called. Her voice trailed away.

He turned on the light in the kitchen. It wasn't much, but it was enough for now. "Want a beer?" he asked, holding his own up in the dim light of the doorway.

"Sure. Why not?"

Well, that was a surprise. He'd figured Lockett would ask for Chardonnay or cabernet. He twisted the top off a bottle and handed it over, noting with grim amusement that she was careful not to actually touch him when she took it.

And then he watched, fascinated, as she tipped it up to her lips and took a long swallow. He saw her tongue flicker out delicately to catch a drop on her bottom lip. Why did her every move have to echo inside him this way? It had been so long, and yet he recognized, remembered, every gesture she made. It was there in the way she bent her wrist, in the way her throat moved ever so slightly when she drank, in the way she tossed back her hair and lifted her chin when she was nervous. It was as if every tiny habit was engraved on his heart.

He wished he didn't remember so clearly. He wished there wasn't so much time and distance between them.

More than either of those, he wished he hadn't kissed her the minute she'd come in the door.

But he'd assumed . . . Clearly, he'd thought all the wrong things.

Closing his heart to a sudden pang of vulnerability, he asked, "Why did you come here? Why did you follow me?"

"I, uh . . ." She licked her lip again, and his gaze was fastened to the motion. "I thought we needed to talk."

He took a long swallow of his own beer. "About what?"

Bracing her back on the wall, Lockett smoothed her white dress over her legs and stared up at the ceiling. "I wanted . . . I wish there could be peace between us." She eyed him warily. "I'm getting married tomorrow—"

"Yeah, I know."

"Well, I would like to do it with a sense of peace." She pulled her long, slim legs underneath her, propping herself up a little higher. "You know, to resolve all the old ugly stuff, so I can go into my new marriage with a clean slate."

"Do you really think that's possible?"

"Why not?"

She always had been a hopeless romantic. "Sure, why not? We'll have a ten-minute chat, we'll pretend nothing ever happened between us, and we can be pals." Ryan shook his head. "Is that what you had in mind?"

"I don't know," she admitted. "I just . . ." She composed her features, carefully casual when she murmured, "I just don't want us to hurt each other anymore."

"Pipe dreams, Lockett."

"No, it's not a pipe dream." She took another long draw on the beer. "Don't you want there to be peace between us? Wouldn't that be preferable to all this sniping and bad feeling?"

"Yes, but—"

"No buts. I've changed," she argued. "I'll bet you have, too. So we can be different people who don't hurt each other anymore. Why not?"

"Because it hurts me just to look at you," he whispered.

Neither tried to comment on that. They retreated to the safety of their beer bottles. "Could I have another, please?" Lockett asked softly.

Ryan looked up. His was only about a quarter gone, and hers was empty? Lockett had changed more than he'd thought. But he got her another bottle, and she took a healthy swig.

"Okay, Lockett, I give," he said finally. "How exactly did you want to go about burying the hatchet here?"

"I don't know," she admitted. "I hadn't thought that far ahead."

"You just followed me with a sort-of-maybe idea that you wanted to talk to me, but you didn't have any idea what you wanted to say?"

"Well, yes." Twisting her hair into a golden knot on top of her head, she sent him a defiant look. "Is that so different from you showing up at my party with some cockamamy story about my father being a crook, or auctioning me off, or whatever you said?"

"I said I didn't have the details—"

"Close enough." She dismissed him with an airy wave of her free hand. "You didn't have a speech put together before you got there, and it showed. I figure you made it all up as you went along. The real truth was that you just wanted to see me."

He choked as beer went down his windpipe. "What?"

"Oh, come on, it's no big deal." She sat up straighter and smiled encouragingly. "I mean, I'm curious about you, too, and what's happened to you since I saw you last. We were important to each other once upon a time. So there's still a certain amount of curiosity there. I just don't feel the need to think up crazy excuses to tell you so."

Trust Lockett to have the most convoluted thinking this side of city hall. "It wasn't an excuse," he insisted. "Your father really is in trouble. Your wedding really is a sham."

"Uh-huh." She tilted up her bottle to get the last drops of beer. "I guess I hadn't realized how thirsty I was," she mused. "Must have been the hors d'oeuvres at that horrid party of Tish Bingwell's. Or maybe the rum drinks. They say rum dries out your mouth, don't they?"

"I wouldn't know."

"Would you be a dear," she asked slowly, with only just a tiny stumble over the words, "and bring me another of these?"

He almost told her she was getting to be a sloppy drunk in her old age, but he refrained. If she wanted to play truth or dare with liquid refreshment, it was no skin off his nose. Besides, he had a sneaky suspicion he might enjoy an advantage in their verbal tennis match if he pushed her a bit further under the influence. So he provided another beer. Thank goodness the fridge was fully stocked when he'd got there.

"So, Lockett," he began. "You're curious about me. Is that what you said?"

"Not exactly." She gave him a funny, measuring look. "But sort of."

Lockett might be too stubborn for her own good when it came to believing what he told her, but Ryan was beginning to enjoy the covetous way she looked at him. Like old times.

"Okay—shoot. What do you want to know?" he asked generously.

"You'll tell me anything I want to know?"

He raised an eyebrow. "Up to a point."

"Okay." She settled in with a certain air of eagerness. "What did you do when I left?"

It wasn't what he'd expected.

"After I tore the place apart?" There wasn't enough booze in the world to dull that pain. "I left. Never went back there."

"Did you look for me?" she asked softly.

"No." He switched the light off in the kitchen. Maybe this conversation was better off completely in the dark after all. "Your father told me where you were. He sent pictures of you. Smiling. Looking very happy. So when he added that I shouldn't contact you, that you'd left of your own free will, I believed it." He took a quick gulp of beer. "I guess."

"It was true," she whispered. "I guess."

Silence hung heavy in the small, humid apartment.

"And what about school?" Lockett asked after a moment.

"What about it?"

"Did you finish? I mean, you were pretty close to your degree when I left."

He sighed. She was dredging up a lot of water he'd thought was safely under the bridge.

"Well?"

Quickly, tersely, he quipped, "Nope. Didn't finish. No point."

"What do you mean?"

"Do I really have to go into this?"

"Yes," she said with a challenge in her voice. "You said you'd answer whatever I asked. We're going for peace, remember? You might as well just get it over with."

"Okay." He shrugged. "I was pre-law, remember?"

"Yes."

"Okay, so I got arrested. There was no point in continuing after that," he said darkly. "You can't take the bar exam when you have a felony conviction on your record. So my legal career was over a long time before it got started."

"Arrested? A felony conviction?" she demanded, obviously shocked. Even in the shadowy light he could see her eyes were round with surprise. "What did you do?"

He lifted his shoulders but didn't respond.

"Uncle Max. Am I right? You were doing some scummy favor for Uncle Max, and the police picked you up?"

She sounded like Lockett on the warpath. He remembered this argument—they'd had it several times.

You can be someone, Tony. But not if you let yourself get tarred with Max Fiorin's brush. Break off the connection now, before it's too late, before you get caught.

And he would tell her that she didn't understand, that Max was family, that it would all work out okay. Too bad she'd been right.

"It was Max, wasn't it?" she repeated.

"Yeah. So that leaves out police work and major league baseball as career choices," he said lightly. "Oh, and maybe President, too. Can you be President if you have a record?"

Lockett ignored the flippant question. "So what did you do?"

"Went back to my first love," he murmured. "Before you."

"A-another woman?" she sputtered.

He laughed at that one. "No, Lockett. Golf. Remember, I was a caddy?"

"So you're telling me that now you're a golf pro?" she asked with obvious disbelief.

"Uh, no, not exactly."

"Oh, Ryan." Unsteadily, she got to her feet, sliding along the wall till she got closer. "Don't tell me you're still a caddy?"

Once again, he choked on his beer. "Something like that," he managed.

"Oh, you're making this up."

She smacked him on the shoulder haphazardly, almost completely missing. He began to get the idea that Lockett was pretty far into her cups. In her usual fashion, she was not showy about it. She just seemed to have acquired a real lack of coordination.

Slumping onto the wall beside him, she slipped a bit more than she'd planned. There was a thud as her shoulder came to a stop, resting hard up against his. Kindly, he steadied her. She peered at him with those round blue eyes.

"Are you moving or am I?"

"Neither."

"That's funny," she mumbled. "I could've sworn one of us was moving."

Ryan just shook his head. "So what about you?"

"Excuse me?" she asked with a delicate hiccup.

"What you do for a living. Your store," he said patiently. "I've seen it from the outside. It's cute."

"It's not cute," she said hotly. She bonked him on the arm with her beer bottle. "It's beautiful. Locketts and Lace." She smiled mistily. "I love it. I sell all kinds of Victorian reproduction clothes. And gloves. And shoes. Oh, and lockets, of course."

She looked like she was going to topple over at any second, so he steered her back into the living room, framing her shoulders with his hands, propping her back against the wall. She looked sleepy and confused. She looked adorable. Oh, well. At least she wasn't hitting or yelling at him.

As soon as his hands released her, she slid back down the wall to a semiseated position. Ryan joined her on the floor, his back next to hers. In the darkness, that seemed to be as good a way as any to carry on a conversation.

"So this business of yours, what does Stanford think of it?"

"Who knows?" Lockett giggled. "That's the beauty of it." She put a finger to her lips and started to whisper loudly. "He's never seen it. Stanford and my parents seem to think it's some kind of toy. You know, something for Lockett to play with. So I can do anything I want with it and nobody bothers me."

"And is that enough?"

"Enough for what?" she asked, confused.

"You always had all those dreams for what you were going to do when you grew up. I just wondered," he asked thoughtfully, "if your Locketts and Lace store was enough to satisfy your dreams?"

"My dreams?" She seemed to be focusing on something up around the ceiling. Her eyes were wide and soft. "I was going to be an artist. Did you know that? I was going to go to Paris and be an artist." She giggled again. "Or at least sleep with an artist. Did you know that?"

"No."

"Yeah, I gave it up when I met you." Her smile wobbled. "You seemed like a better dream at the time."

"Or maybe just a more convenient way to get out from under your father's thumb?"

She considered. "Maybe."

He didn't want to think their time together had been based on that, but he knew that was at least part of the equation. And when living with him had become more of a burden, then back she went to Daddy. Escaping from one to the other. Not a pretty picture.

"Tony?" Lockett asked drowsily.

He almost didn't answer. Nobody had called him that in years. It was pretty painful hearing it now, from her lips. But he said, "Yeah?"

"You really are nice, you know that?"

"No, I'm not," he muttered.

But Lockett's head was lodged against his shoulder. Her hair drifted, fine and shiny, down his arm.

"Lockett?" he tried.

No answer. She was clearly asleep.

With a heavy sigh, Ryan bent over and hoisted her up into his arms. His conversation was so diverting that his ex-bride had decided to take a nap on the floor. Other than roaring up to the Kensington mansion and dumping her on the doorstep, he had no choice but to put her to bed and let her sleep it off.

In his bed.

"Well, this ought to put a crimp in the wedding plans," he said out loud.

"You're so nice," she breathed into his ear.

"No," he repeated. He slipped her down onto the bed and reached for her top button. "I'm not that nice."

Chapter Five

Floral Fantasy

The scent of flowers was overpowering. Carnations, maybe, and lilies, with a heady undercurrent of roses.

Lockett dreamed she was romping in a field of flowers, naked as the day she was born. She and Ryan were making love, carelessly rolling in the flowers, crushing the fragrant blooms with the weight of their passion.

"Mmm," she murmured. It was so real, she could hear his heartbeat and smell the earthy, sweat-glazed scent of his body mixed with all those lovely flowers.

Amazingly real. She raised her head sleepily, groping for the alarm clock that sat next to her bed. But, aside from the terrible pounding headache that seemed to have arisen out of nowhere, all she discovered was a mouth. A mouth? Her fingers had closed over a warm, breathing mouth.

Her eyes shot open. There was a man beside her in the bed.

She must be hallucinating.

She sat up so abruptly she almost lost the dark maroon plaid sheet that covered her. Maroon? But her bed was positively dripping in white lace. She didn't have any dark sheets.

Bed linens were the least of her problems at the moment. She was almost naked, wearing nothing but a very small pair of panties, and she was in bed, a strange one, next to...

Next to Antonio Ryan. Her ex-husband.

While he slept on, oblivious, she was experiencing cardiac arrest.

"Oh, my God," she whispered. "What have I done?"

But her pounding head yielded no answers. Maybe that was a good sign. Surely she'd remember if she'd... if they'd...

"Oh, no," she moaned, ducking back under the covers. But they couldn't have. If she'd made love with Ryan, if it had been anything like it was in the old days, she would definitely have remembered.

On the other hand, if she'd really done it, really gone and done what she'd been thinking about nonstop for eight years, and now she couldn't even remember—well, she was going to kill herself.

"We didn't do it," she said fiercely.

They'd talked. That much she could remember. Snippets of conversation. It was murky, but it was there.

Okay, what else?

Beer. She'd had a couple of beers. She'd felt safe, warm, expansive.

"Oh, God." That didn't sound good at all. Safe, warm, in the mood for... "I couldn't have."

And then it hit her. She was supposed to get married today.

She took a shallow breath. She was supposed to get married *to someone else*.

Responsible, well-bred young women didn't do this sort of thing. Even if nothing had happened—and she prayed that it hadn't—spending the night with someone other than one's fiancé on the eve of one's wedding was positively *seedy*. Lockett squeezed her eyes shut, trying not to think about it.

"Lockett?" Ryan mumbled. "Are you awake?"

"Uh, no," she said shakily. "I mean, yes. Are you?"

She was trying to stay safely on her side of the bed, with a lot of bedclothes between them. What was he wearing under there? As little as she was? *And what had happened to her clothes?*

"Cooler this morning. Front must've come through." He sat up in the bed, stretching luxuriously, and she couldn't stop her gaze from wandering down the expanse of his firmly muscled torso, down to where a dark vee of hair disappeared into the bedclothes.

"Oh, God," she whispered. Divine intervention seemed to be her only hope at this point, not that she deserved it. She raised a weak hand to her forehead. "Uh, Ryan, do you know what happened to my clothes?"

He blinked. And then he smiled. She didn't like the look of that smile. "Wondering what happened last night, are we?"

"No, of course not." She felt her cheeks flush with color. "Of course I know what happened last night. It was, um, after my bachelorette party. And I, uh, came here. And we talked..."

"And then..."

"And then?" she asked anxiously. "What then?"

Ryan leaned over closer, negligently letting the sheet gap even more. She squeezed her eyes shut. "And then..." he whispered, his breath soft and warm against her cheek. "And then... Nothing."

She opened one eye. "Nothing?"

"Oh, come on, Lockett." He tossed the covers aside as he jumped out of bed and strode for the bathroom. He was wearing boxers. Thank God. "You had too much to drink, so I put you to bed. End of story."

"End of story?" She was so relieved she collapsed back onto the bed.

"Well, I did take off your dress." He frowned. "The buttons on the back were really a pain, and I had to rip it to get it off. Sorry."

"You ripped my dress?" she asked, aghast. It was bad enough that he'd taken it off, but did he have to ruin it, too? "Why couldn't you leave me asleep in my dress?"

"You know, Lockett, that never occurred to me." With his hand on the door to the bathroom, he smiled. "Don't worry. You haven't got anything I haven't seen before."

"I know," she said gloomily as she tried to rouse herself from this amazing depression.

She should be jumping with joy she hadn't slept with the man. But she was swamped with depression.

She should be happy. She was supposed to get married in a few hours. And yet here she was, unclothed and miserable, in someone else's bed. She heard the splash of Ryan's shower, and she hopped out of bed quickly, intent on getting up and out of there before he came back.

Maybe everything would still be okay if she could just get home and get a cup of black coffee.

"Dress," she mumbled, dragging along a sheet for protection. "I need my dress."

After all, how bad could it be? Terrible, she realized when she found it in a heap next to the bed. He had ripped the back open completely. And she could hardly prance home in a dress that wouldn't stay on.

"All right, then, Mr. Smarty Pants Ex-husband," she said to herself. "We'll just take your clothes."

So she rummaged through Ryan's drawers until she found a black T-shirt—identical to the one he'd had on last night—and a pair of silk pajama bottoms still in the box.

"Perfect," she said, hoisting the bottoms up at the drawstring waist. "Although I can't believe Ryan has silk pajamas. When he was with me, he never slept in anything but skin—"

Ryan in the buff was not what she needed to be thinking about right now.

Just as she pulled on the makeshift outfit, she heard a voice out in the main part of the apartment.

"Hello? Ryan? You up?"

And then a man barged right into the bedroom, where Lockett was hastily tucking the T-shirt into her pants.

"Oh, hi," he said easily. He was as tall as Ryan, a bit darker, and very handsome, in a way that was almost too polished. She knew him.

"You're—" she began.

"Joey," he supplied. "Ryan's cousin."

Joey Fiorin. The son of Max Fiorin, crime boss of the west side. Joey wasn't really Ryan's cousin, but since they'd grown up together, everybody had long since forgotten there was no blood relation.

"We've, uh, met," she managed. "Way back when. I used to be married to Ryan."

"Oh." He peered closer. "Sure. Lockett. You look different. Must be the outfit."

Just as she was about to ask what he was doing barging into the middle of Ryan's bedroom uninvited, Ryan himself strolled out of the bathroom wearing nothing but a towel. Oh, heavens. He looked spectacular. Lockett forced herself to look somewhere else.

"Hey," Ryan announced, "what are you doing here, Joey?"

"Dad asked me to come by."

"Ever learn to knock?" Ryan asked shortly.

Joey shrugged inside his expensive suit. "I've got a key. It's a good place, y'know. With the flower shop downstairs. Convenient."

"Flower shop downstairs?" Lockett echoed.

"Fiorin Flowers." Joey grinned. "Maybe you've heard of it?"

Oh, yeah, she'd heard of it. In the old days Fiorin Flowers provided the funeral wreaths for all the gangsters in town. Rumor was they'd do it free if they'd knocked off the guy in the casket.

So Ryan was ensconced in an apartment right above the famous Fiorin flower shop.

"Uncle Max loan you this place?" she asked slowly.

"Yes, but—" Ryan began.

Joey cut him off, tapping him on the arm. "Listen, Ryan, Max needs a meeting. You on?"

Ryan's brows lowered. "Maybe. When?"

Lockett noticed that, all Ryan's protests aside, when Max Fiorin asked for a meeting, he didn't say no.

"Now. Right away," Joey told him. His gaze flickered over Lockett. "She safe?"

"Not really."

Her suspicions were growing stronger by the minute. Hadn't Ryan told her that he didn't have anything to do with the Fiorin family anymore? Hadn't getting arrested on their behalf and losing his chance to be a lawyer taught him a lesson?

Apparently not. He lived in their apartment, his cousin had a key, and when Uncle Max wanted to meet, Ryan was in. Not good at all.

"It's, uh, about that business you previously discussed," Joey continued. "Something's come up."

"Can't make it right now." Ryan reached for a T-shirt from the drawer. "I'm busy."

Joey smiled. "Yeah, well, I can see that. But sometimes business before pleasure, you know what I mean?"

He meant *her*. Lockett crossed her arms over her borrowed T-shirt, not liking any of this one bit.

"Don't mind me," she said. "I was just leaving."

But Ryan caught her arm. "Where are you going?"

"I'm getting married in a few hours, remember?" she inquired. "I'd better hit the road."

"But after last night—"

"Nothing happened last night," she said quickly. She shook away his hand. "You said so, didn't you?"

"You can't marry him, Lockett."

"Oh, yes, I can."

With every scrap of dignity she could muster, given the fact that she was wearing a T-shirt down to her knees and pajama bottoms trailing the floor, she stepped out of Ryan's apartment.

She shut the door quietly, and then hotfooted it down the stairs, jumping into her Porsche and roaring out of there before he had a chance to follow.

LOCKETT PULLED HER CAR up around to the kitchen driveway. It was almost ten, and she fully expected servants to be running around like crazy getting ready for the wedding. But it was still safer to go in the back than risk the front door.

She could hear the conversation now.

Hello, Mother. Why am I just now getting home? Why am I dressed so strangely? It's really very simple— You see, I was attacked by a wayward band of grunge musicians and they forced me to stay out all night and wear their clothes...

No, she couldn't tangle with her parents just yet. Which meant sneaking around the outside of her own house, looking like some kind of bizarre pajama-clad burglar.

But she had to get in there somehow. And the less conspicuous she was about it, the better.

Feeling like an idiot, she put on her sunglasses, shook her hair down around her face—as if either of those maneuvers would really fool anyone—and stealthily crept over to the kitchen door. Thank goodness things were pretty quiet at the moment. No one was around but Cook, whose ample behind was visible at the far end of the kitchen. Lockett could see her over by the refrigerator, where it appeared she was working up some sort of special breakfast tray.

Meanwhile, Lockett's wedding cake stood, in all its five-tiered glory, on the kitchen's center island.

Her wedding cake. She felt a lump in her throat. It was beautiful, everything she had imagined when she'd pored through books and brainstormed with Monsieur Jean-Jacques, the designer. Instead of bright white, she'd gone for a pale, cream-colored icing, with cascading roses and ropes of pearls in marzipan. Most of the flowers were done in the same creamy white or pale vanilla, with one or two in blush pink to show off Monsieur Jean-Jacques's artistry.

It was a masterpiece, truly worthy of the wedding of the year. But if Lockett didn't sneak herself in that house and behave like some semblance of a bride within the next ten minutes, neither the cake nor the wedding would be going anywhere.

"Come on, Cook," she muttered under her breath. "Get the breakfast tray and get out of there."

Lockett hovered there at the kitchen window, waiting for her opportunity. Finally, after spiking a glass of tomato juice with a fat stalk of celery, Cook gathered up her tray and ambled out the swinging doors.

There was no time to waste. Lockett raced in and bolted up the servants' staircase without pausing to take a breath. With plush carpet under her feet and cool air wafting from every register, it felt great to be home. And after a close call with one of the maids, she managed to tiptoe through the upstairs parlor and make it down the hall to her own bedroom.

So far, so good. With victory at hand, she turned the knob. But the door was locked. Her own bedroom door was locked from the inside.

Lockett tried the handle again. No good.

"Who is it?" a voice whispered from inside.

Beatie. Lockett sighed with relief. She didn't know why her little sister had locked the door, but at least she could be trusted not to go blabbing about the shape the bride was in just hours before the wedding.

"Beatie, it's me," Lockett whispered back. "Open up."

"Where have you been?" Beatie demanded as she whipped open the door and stepped back to let her sister enter. "I've been holding down the fort telling everyone you wanted to sleep late, but it's almost ten o'clock, Lockett! I wasn't sure how much longer I was going to be able to keep it up. And *besides,* you abandoned me at that *horrid* party last night. I had to get a ride home from Muffin and Gigi, and they were both insufferable. You should've seen Muffin pawing the stripper—the real stripper, I mean—not Ryan, although she would've pawed him, too, if he would've stuck around—"

"Beatie, are you ever going to take a breath?"

"Sorry." She fixed wide eyes on Lockett's unorthodox outfit. "Where have you been? What happened to you?"

Before Lockett had a chance to open her mouth, Beatie gasped out loud.

Circling her disheveled sister, she declared, "Oh, my God, Lockett! Tell me you didn't!"

"Didn't what?" she asked weakly.

"You were with Ryan, weren't you?" Beatie's mouth curved into a satisfied smile. "You sly dog. I knew you both disappeared about the same time, but I never thought... Oh, happy day! You slept with Ryan—now you can't marry the twit!"

"I didn't..." She faltered for just a second. "Nothing happened between me and Ryan. I mean, I spent the night with him, but not in *that way*. So nothing happened. Well, almost nothing. And Stanford doesn't ever have to know."

Beatie's jaw dropped. "You mean you really *did* sleep with Ryan?" she squealed. "I can't believe it! I was just kidding."

"Could you keep your voice down, please? I said I didn't sleep with Ryan, didn't I?"

"Oh, my God, Lockett! I can't believe this." Beatie whirled around in a wide arc. "You actually *did it.* With Ryan." She clapped a hand over her mouth. "This is so cool. Things are really going to pick up now. When do the fireworks start?"

Lockett was too exhausted and too confused to figure out Beatie's train of thought. "Fireworks? What are you talking about?" she asked, already pulling off the pieces of her horrible escape outfit and reaching for her robe.

"You. Ryan. The wedding. Everything is up for grabs." Beatie giggled. "I can't wait to see Stanford's face when you tell him. I can't wait to see *Daddy's* face, when he has to tell all the guests to go home. This is going to be such fun!"

"Beatie!" Lockett kicked the pajama bottoms and T-shirt under her bed. "Will you please keep it down? Anyone walking down the hall could hear you. And I don't know where you got the idea I wasn't going through with the wedding. I told you, nothing happened."

"No!" Beatie shrieked. "You can't do that. You're supposed to be making plans to run off with Ryan. You can't get married!"

"Well, I certainly can't run off with Ryan." Lockett forced herself to maintain a calm exterior, even though her stomach was churning and she had a headache the size of Lake Michigan. "Ryan is the same person he always was, and I don't get along very well with that person. We spent the night together purely by accident and it doesn't mean anything."

"But, Lockett... You can't go through with the wedding. Not now."

"Oh, yes, I can." Taking a deep breath, Lockett tied the sash on her robe and made a beeline for the bathroom. "Call down and get Cook to send up a tray, will you? I need coffee and a glass of tomato juice, maybe a croissant if she has one. But lots of coffee, black." Halfway to the door to her bath, she turned back. "On second thought, forget the tomato juice. Make it a Bloody Mary. I need the vodka."

"Lockett." Her sister tried again. "You cannot go through with the wedding. It isn't right!"

"Beatie, I really don't have time for this. My hairdresser should be here any minute. And the dressing assistants from the designer, too. Where's my wedding dress?" She cast an anxious glance around the room. "Isn't my dress supposed to be here?"

"It's right there." Heaving a huge sigh, Beatie swung open the door to Lockett's walk-in closet, revealing a long dress bag that hung on the back of the door. "I saw you put it there yesterday. Before the stupid bachelorette party. *Before* Ryan walked in and you walked out. *Before* you slept with him!"

Lockett's head was pounding. She released a sigh of her own. "What exactly is your problem? How many times do I have to tell you I didn't sleep with him?"

"You can't say it enough times for me to believe you." After slamming the closet door, Beatie turned back to face her sister. "And even if you didn't go through with *the act*, it's the same problem. You love Ryan. And you can't marry Stanford if you don't love him."

"Why not?" she demanded. "People do it all the time."

"So you admit you don't love him?" Beatie asked triumphantly.

"No, I don't." She raised a hand to her head. "I mean, yes, I do. Love him. I'm just..." *Oh, dear.* The realization hit her with the force of a nuclear blast. "I'm just..."

"Not in love with him," Beatie finished for her. "Exactly. So, are you the moral, responsible, role model I know and respect, the person who would never consider saying 'I do' to a man she doesn't love?"

"But how can I—"

"How can you go through with this, with Stanford in the dark about something very important? Don't you think he might care that you saw your ex-husband last night, that you spent the night with him?"

"Yes, I do," she cried. "But that's exactly why I can't tell him."

"Far be it from me to defend Stanford Marsh." Under her breath, Beatie added, "Who is a first-class ninny as far as I can make out. But somebody has to tell you that it isn't fair to Stanford, and it certainly isn't fair to Ryan, for you to still have feelings for one man and marry the other one!"

Lockett slumped against the bathroom door. It wasn't bad enough that she was doing a terrific job of making a hash of her life—now her annoying little sister had to hit her over the head with it. "But I'm not in love with Ryan," she ventured, feeling very confused. "It's just old embers. You know, that kind of thing. No open flames."

"Oh, right! Do you expect me to believe that?"

"Yes!" Lockett declared. "I do!"

"I hope that's the last time you say 'I do' today," Beatie said hotly. "Calling off the wedding is your only choice."

"Let me get this straight—it's better to break Stanford's heart by telling him the truth and calling the whole thing off than it is to keep one little secret and go through with it?"

"Exactly!"

"Beatie, give me a break. I'm not in love with Ryan!"

"But you do have doubts about Stan?"

"Well, yes, but—"

"Then you can't do it!" Beatie finished. "You absolutely can't!"

"Beatrice, are you bothering your sister?" asked Marjorie Kensington as she angled her elegant blond head around the bedroom door. "Good morning, children. Lockett, darling, I'm glad to see you've finally consented to join the land of the living, but, darling, you're ages behind schedule. Do pop in and get your bath, sweetheart. Mr. André is already downstairs waiting to get his hands on your hair. And Beatrice, it's past time you were off starting your own toilette."

As Mrs. Kensington took her younger daughter by the arm and propelled her out of the room, Beatie turned back with a very determined expression. "Think about what I said, Lockett. Think about it before you do something you will really regret. I know you'll do the right thing before it's too late. Just *think* about it, okay?"

She didn't have much choice. No matter what she did, no matter how long she languished in the bathtub, her mind kept turning her dilemma over and over again. What was fair? What was right? What should she do?

As she was hustled out of the tub and into her role as bride-to-be, Lockett barely noticed what was happening. She sat obediently as Mr. André fretted over her hair and a manicurist fussed with the nails that some ten hours ago had been raking down Ryan's back. As three dresser's assistants wrapped her in this and that, she stumbled blindly along for the ride.

Somehow, she was dressed and coiffed. Somehow, she was bound into all the appropriate accoutrements, from sheer stockings and French-heeled shoes to her grandmother's pearl-and-diamond earrings, from the yards of lace and satin weighing down her skirt, to the pouf and drape of her elaborate veil.

When she looked in the mirror, she saw the perfect bride. Except for the eyes. There was an eerie light in her eyes that spoke volumes about pure terror.

"Lovely," Mr. André said as he stuck in the last pin on her veil. "Simply lovely."

"Lovely," echoed one of the dressers who'd buttoned Lockett into the impossible dress.

"Exquisite," offered Marjorie Kensington, shooing out the others. She came back in to stand at Lockett's shoulder, fluffing the veil and beaming at her daughter's reflection.

Lockett couldn't take her eyes off the vision in the mirror. *Beauty is as beauty does,* she thought. *You as good as betrayed your groom and you're not even married to him yet.*

She began to panic. Was Beatie right? Was it worse to marry poor Stanford, knowing in her heart that she wasn't sure she loved him, than it was to publicly humiliate all of them by calling off the wedding?

The heavy dress, with its boned bodice and four separate petticoats, felt like an instrument of torture. The pins and combs in the veil pressed against her scalp.

Lockett was absolutely and completely miserable, racked with guilt, torn with indecision.

"Mother," she said suddenly. "What if I want to call off the wedding?"

Chapter Six

Bridal Bliss

"Don't be ridiculous." Marjorie Kensington smiled indulgently. "A few jitters, darling? Nothing to worry about."

"This isn't jitters, Mother. This is serious." She could hear the note of hysteria dancing around the edge of her voice.

"Lockett," her mother said more sternly. "Don't be absurd. Now calm down, darling. Everything will be just fine."

"Mother—"

"I won't hear any more of this." Her tone grew chillier. "Your father would be very upset if he knew you were behaving this way. I don't have to tell you that this wedding is very important to him, Lockett. Throwing up obstacles at this late date is maddeningly inappropriate."

"Mother, believe me, I wouldn't be bringing this up if it weren't extremely important." Her mind was racing. How could she go into a church and promise to honor and to cherish and all that stuff if she wasn't sure? The more she considered it, the more she thought about standing next to Stanford, taking vows, promising to God and everyone that she would love, honor and obey... the more she wanted to jump out the window and be done with it. "Stanford. That's it!"

He was the one who should make the decision. Go on? Or quit now? Only he could decide. She would tell him how she felt, that she had spent the night with Ryan, even though nothing had happened. If he still wanted to go on with it, knowing that, then so be it. Lockett felt better already.

"Mother, please, go get Stanford. I need to see him right away."

"Darling, you're being ridiculous." Mrs. Kensington sent her daughter a disapproving frown. "You can't see the groom an hour before the wedding."

"I have to see him."

"I won't hear of it."

"Mother, please. Get Stanford for me."

"Absolutely not."

But Lockett was just panicky enough not to give in. "If you won't bring him up here, then I'll go down." She began to gather up her skirts.

"You will not go down and see him. I already told you, the groom can't see the bride before the wedding. What is wrong with you?" Her mother's voice rose dramatically. "Lockett, stop that! You'll wrinkle your gown!"

She sighed, releasing the handfuls of fabric she was holding. "Beatie, then. Get Beatie. I can see my own sister, can't I?"

"Lockett," her mother said in a very ominous tone. "You will see Beatrice when we get to the church. Pull yourself together."

But Lockett wasn't going to be budged. "Get Beatie."

They glared at each other for a long moment.

"All right," Marjorie said finally. "I don't suppose it will hurt anything if I let you talk to Beatrice for a moment. But no more of these games, Lockett. As soon as you two have your little tête-à-tête, we must get off to the church. Your father will be furious we're behind schedule."

But Lockett had learned how to maintain a haughty attitude at her mother's knee. Chin up, trying to keep her entire body from trembling, she announced, "I really don't think Daddy will mind waiting a few minutes once he knows his daughter's entire future happiness depends upon it."

"Don't be tiresome, darling. It doesn't become you."

But off she went to find Beatie.

Although Lockett was even more skittish than she'd been when she'd started, the battle with her mother had only strengthened her resolve. She had no intention of carrying on as planned until things were settled to her satisfaction. And that meant talking things through with her fiancé.

Beatie came running through the door, lifting the abundant skirts of her pale yellow maid-of-honor dress in front of her so she didn't trip. "What is it? Mother is furious! Are you calling it off?"

"Yes ... no ... I don't know," she managed. "But I need to see Stanford. Only, Mother refused to go get him. Is he here in the house? Can you find him, Beatie?"

"Well, yes, he is here. He and Father were having a toast or something in the study, I think, but his limo is supposed to leave any second." Beatie wrung her hands.

"But why do you want to see him? And how am I supposed to get him up here without Mother seeing him?"

"I don't care. Just do it." She took her sister's hands in her own. "Beatie, please, this is important."

"Lockett, your hands are freezing. Are you ill? If you fainted or something, we might be able to get them to at least postpone it."

"I think Mother would just prop me up and say 'I do' for me," Lockett muttered.

"Don't move. I'll get Stan the Man."

"Thanks, Beatie," she called after her. And then she paced back and forth until she heard soft footfalls headed down the hall.

Here comes the groom . . .

Beatie ushered him in and then ran back out again. "I'll be out in the hall if you need me," she said helpfully.

Lockett nodded. But she was gazing woefully at her fiancé, wondering how in the world she was going to broach this.

Stanford's color was high, and his formal collar looked a bit tight under his ascot. He was a tall, rather thin man, and he looked very nice in a cutaway and waistcoat. Not terribly exciting, but distinguished, as if he could step into a role as vice president of a bank, or perhaps a junior senator, without raising a sweat on his high, noble forehead.

"This is very strange, Lockett," he began. "You know the bride and groom aren't supposed to see each other before the wedding."

She sighed and sat down on the bed, squashing the back of her wedding gown. "Yes, I know. My mother's been telling me for the last hour."

"Stand up, dear. You'll mess your dress," he said. Concern for her pristine appearance furrowed his brow.

She stayed where she was. "Stanford, what I have to say is more important than a few wrinkles."

"You think so now," he said kindly, taking her elbow and hoisting her to her feet. "But when you're standing at the altar with a rumpled dress in full view of the congregation, I think you'll feel differently."

"But that's what I'm trying to tell you," she persisted. "I'm just not sure I have any business standing at the altar."

"What is that supposed to mean?"

"That I'm not sure I can marry you," she said in a rush. "I'm sorry, Stanford, but I'm just not sure."

"I'm sure enough for both of us." He smiled encouragingly. "All right, then. Was that it? Just a little reassurance, eh? I'll go back down before your mother catches us, and I'll see you at the church."

He bent to kiss her on the cheek, but Lockett backed away. "No, no, that's not it. I don't need a little reassurance. I need to speak with you."

"Nothing you can say will change my mind, dear."

"But you don't even know what's bothering me yet."

"It won't matter," he assured her. "I'm positive of that."

She felt like stamping her foot. Was there no one who would take her seriously and actually hear what she had to say? "Stanford, I am not leaving this room until you listen to me."

He heaved an impatient sigh. Carefully arranging the tails on his jacket so that they didn't get mussed, Stanford sat down on the settee opposite her bed. "Well?"

Lockett paced off a line in front of him. Rubbing her hands together, debating how exactly to start, she finally said, "It's my ex-husband." She glanced up. "I did tell you I was married before, didn't I?"

"I don't recall if you did or not, but your father did warn me that the fellow in question might present a problem."

"My father..." Lockett was aghast. Why would her father say anything to Stanford about Ryan?

"So the ex has shown up and caused trouble, has he? Is that why you're worried?" Stanford stood and smoothed his tails. "Don't worry, darling. Elliot warned me. I gather he's had this guy—Ryan, isn't it?— followed of late just to be sure. He was considering having someone keep an eye on you, too, keep you out of the guy's way in case of trouble, but I didn't feel that was necessary. As a matter of fact, I talked him out of it. So I'm afraid if the ex has shown up and bothered you, it's really my fault, as well." He smiled apologetically. "I called off the dogs, as it were."

She hadn't absorbed any of this yet. She was still trying to take in the fact that her father was considering having her followed. Just to keep Ryan away from her.

Ryan's voice echoed inside her head.

Why is your father so afraid you won't go through with it that he resorts to a crazy tactic like coming after me after all these years? What does he have to lose? Ask yourself that, Lockett. Why is your dad so hot to marry you off to Stanford Marsh?

"Wh-why would he do that?" she whispered. "Why would he send someone to follow Ryan? Or follow me?"

"To make sure nothing interferes with the wedding, of course," Stanford returned easily.

"'To make sure nothing interferes with the wedding...'"

Why is your dad so hot to marry you off to Stanford Marsh?

Why? She had no idea. She only knew she was going to scream if something didn't start to make sense.

"But what if something does interfere with the wedding?" she inquired quickly.

"Nothing will. Your father and I won't allow it."

"Allow it?" Why did she suddenly feel about ten years old? Where had all these men come from all of a sudden, allowing this and not allowing that? Angrily, she returned, "But there are many things neither you nor my father can control. What if *I* don't want to go through with it? What if I can't?"

"Don't be silly, darling." He practically patted her on the head. "You can. You will."

"I can't."

"Of course you can." Stanford rose and turned to go. "See you at the church."

"Stanford, listen to me." She was desperate to make him understand the depth of their problem. "Ryan didn't bother me or threaten me, or whatever you think."

His hand on the knob, Stanford didn't turn back. "Yes?" he prompted.

She had no choice; she had to spill the whole, ugly thing. Quietly, quickly, she confessed, "He didn't bother me—he came to see me. And I went home with him. I mean, I spent the night with him. Last night. I mean..."

Her fiancé went very still.

"Nothing happened. Nothing really. But I'm not sure other people would see it that way. If anyone saw me, and you found out later where I'd been, well, I would hate that.'' She rushed on. "I'm sorry to just blurt it out like this, but I had to make you see what was wrong. You had to know, so that you could back out, if you needed to. I'll understand completely...."

But he said nothing.

"Oh, Stanford, I'm so sorry. It was just that I saw him, unexpectedly, and we have this history..." His back was rigid. But it was easier to talk to his back than to face him. "I told you, nothing happened. At least, I'm pretty sure nothing happened. I mean, I was there, and he was there, and we slept in the same bed, but that is absolutely all it was. It wasn't anything anyone planned—it just happened. But now you see why I was so upset, why I thought perhaps we should cancel the wedding."

Stanford turned. He looked a little stiff, but otherwise all right. On his face, she read no hysterics, no heartbreak, not even any anger or surprise.

Maybe he was in shock. "I'm sorry," she tried again. She lifted a hand to her head, but she hit the crown of her headdress so firmly attached up there. Damn this wedding and all the paraphernalia attached to it.

Still, Stanford said nothing.

Lockett rambled on, saying whatever came to her mind to fill the space. "I know this is going to be difficult, but I'm starting to think the only thing we can do is to put everything on hold. We can say I have pneumonia or something, just to give me time to figure it all out. I don't know—I don't think I'm still in love with him. But what if I am? And what do I feel for you? I thought I loved you—I still do. But it's such a crazy thing with Ryan, this history we have...."

Finally, Stanford spoke. "I don't see why this has to affect our plans at all," he said calmly. "You made a mistake. You made an unfortunate choice. But I forgive you. 'Nuff said."

"*'Nuff said?*" She was floored. "Your fiancé spends the night with another man the night before your wedding, then comes back and tells you she's not sure she loves you, and all you can say is ''Nuff said'?"

"I prefer not to make a big deal of this." He shrugged. "We'll just pretend it never happened." Glancing at his watch, he added, "Almost show time. We'd better make tracks."

"I can't—" She tried, but he was already out the door. "Is he numb? Or does he just not care?"

Beatie poked her head in. "Everything okay? Are we on or off?"

"I told him, Beatie— I told him about Ryan," Lockett declared with growing incredulity. "He didn't turn an eyelash. Do you believe it? I don't think it mattered to him at all."

"I told you he was a twit."

"I think maybe you were right." And she was thinking someone else was right, as well. Ryan. All his talk about business mergers and bartered brides began to sound more and more like the truth. Surely any groom who loved his bride would react *somehow* when she told him she was very close to unfaithful.

"So are we on or off?"

"We are definitely off," she said with conviction. "I couldn't possibly marry him now. I mean, if he hadn't wanted to go through with it, I would've understood. But this... this indifference, why it's insulting!" Picking up speed, Lockett turned to her sister. "Beatie, help me out of this dress, will you? Just get the buttons on the back started—there are about eight hundred of them. And then we'll have to get Mother up here to decide who's going to make the announcement and what they're going to say—"

"Lockett," her father bellowed, crashing in the door. "What in the name of all that's holy do you think you're doing?"

"Calling off my wedding," she said as coolly as she could manage. "Would you like to make the announcement or should I?"

"Nobody is making any announcements."

He scowled at her from beneath heavy brows. He was only an inch or two taller than she was, but he had a very intimidating presence. Nonetheless, Lockett held her ground.

"Beatie, help me with this dress, will you?"

"Beatrice," her father countermanded, "out. Now."

Flashing her sister an apologetic look, Beatie scrambled for the door. Lockett couldn't really blame her younger sister. She'd never stood up to him when she was seventeen, either.

"I know this is unpleasant, and somewhat embarrassing, but we'll weather it," Lockett ventured. "Come on, Dad. You have to understand— I simply can't do this."

He dismissed her objections with the wave of one hand. "You will do it. You don't have a choice."

She shook her head, trying to at least get the enormous veil off if she couldn't manage the gown. "There's nothing you can do to force me. I mean, I have to be the one to walk down the aisle and say the words. If I refuse, I refuse. What can you do?"

"Don't be ridiculous," he barked. His face took on a redder hue. "I don't think you realize how important this is."

"I don't think you realize that it's *my* wedding," she said uneasily. She couldn't recall ever seeing her father like this, glassy-eyed and strange, as if he were a general in the midst of a war and she were some poor foot soldier who wouldn't obey orders.

"Do you really think you can beat me at this game?"

"This is no game. This is my life!" she cried.

"This is a disaster. There must be a way..." He mopped his brow, huffing a little as he stalked back and forth in front of the door. "I will not," he blustered, "will *not,* allow you to ruin this for me, do you hear? Nor will I allow you to overturn my plans. This alliance is going to go through whether you like it or not!"

"Alliance?" And Ryan had called it a merger. The unease she'd been feeling escalated into a five-alarm fire. "Is that what this is, some business deal concocted between you and Stanford, with me as some sort of stock offering?"

But he waved that off, too. "Semantics. All marriages are mergers, alliances, partnerships, whatever you want to call it."

"I don't think so."

He glared at her. "I can post a guard at this door within five minutes. I can hold out as long as you can. You can either march out that door and down the aisle now, or I can lock you in here until you see things more clearly."

"This is outrageous." Had the entire world gone crazy since midnight last night? Her father had never spoken to her like this in her entire life—well, not since the episode with Ryan when she was seventeen, anyway—and she simply didn't know how to react. "You would really lock me in here like a prisoner? Your own daughter? Do you hear what you're saying? Daddy, what is wrong with you? You can't do this!"

"Damn right I can."

Lockett raised her chin. "I will not marry Stanford. I will not be the booby prize in a business deal."

"You'll come around," he shouted. "You have to."

And her father stalked out the door, slamming it so loudly the sound reverberated in the corridor for several seconds.

But what was she supposed to do now? She whipped open the door, coming face to face with her sister.

"Beatie, I have to get out of here," she said wildly. "He said he's bringing a guard back to keep me in my room. There may still be time to get out before—"

But heavy footsteps were already tromping up the stairs.

"The servants' stairs." She tried, but even a step in that direction revealed her mother and Stanford, their heads together in some sort of confab, blocking any exit.

She was trapped.

"Help me," she pleaded. And then she jumped back inside her room and bolted the door.

But what was she going to do?

THE PRINCESS was imprisoned in a tower. High up in an ivy-covered dormitory, Lockett gazed out her small window.

It was fall in Maine, and the leaves on the trees outside, swaying over the extensive grounds of the Adams Academy, were quite lovely.

But who saw the leaves? She was miserable. She hated her father. She was dying for Ryan.

The only news she'd had was from her little sister. Beatie was heavily into Nancy Drew at that point, and she kept writing cryptic messages about her friends "Caddy" and "Gardner" and what they were up to. From that Lockett surmised that Beatie had gotten word to Ryan, and that he knew where she was.

Every night she tried to send him telepathic messages. *Come for me... Rescue me... I need you...*

But there was no sign of Ryan. Several months passed. Lockett fell deeper into despair.

Until one night in November, when she stood again at her window, staring into the trees.

From out of nowhere the growl of a motorcycle broke the stillness. A man dressed all in black blasted into sight, riding not on a road but over the rolling hills of the Adams Academy. "Lockett!" he cried from down below her window. "Lockett!"

And her heart stood still.

He dumped the motorcycle, rushing to the vines, looking for handholds and a way up to her. Without a second's hesitation Lockett threw a coat over her nightgown and climbed out the window.

They met about fifteen feet off the ground, and in their haste to kiss and get their arms around each other, they almost fell a few times.

But finally they stumbled back to the bike. She clambered on behind him and they roared off together into the darkness.

THINK ABOUT WHO always comes to your rescue when you need it the most...

Lockett raced over to the window, grabbing handfuls of her skirt as she ran.

But she had no sooner swung it open than a lean, gorgeous face appeared above the sill. Lockett fell backward in surprise.

"I've been out here clinging to a vine for ten minutes," Ryan said darkly as he heaved himself up and over, into her bedroom. "What took you so long?"

Chapter Seven

Honeymoon Havens

"H-how did you get there?"

"Your sister called me. It appears I'm supposed to rescue you." He shook his head in mock aggravation. "Again. Although why the hell I keep doing this is beyond me."

But Lockett wasn't in the mood for more fights. She grabbed him and kissed him quick. "I've never been more happy to see anyone in my entire life. Get me out of here, will you?"

"Happy to oblige." Without further ado, he hoisted her up in the air and slung her over one shoulder.

"Do we have to do it this way?" she asked, bumping and thumping up there as he carefully maneuvered them back out the window.

"It's the only way I can climb and carry you at the same time," he muttered. "Pipe down and lie still, or I'll have to knock you out."

"You wouldn't—"

But he was already descending slowly, climbing down the trellis. Lockett squeezed her eyes closed as the ground approached. This sort of thing had seemed a lot more romantic when she was seventeen.

Finally, after an eternity on the damn trellis, he set her on the ground. "Let's go," he ordered, clutching at her hand and heading for his motorcycle. "Run for it. We have to be long gone before they discover you're missing."

The terrible irony of it did not escape her. Once more she would be running off into the unknown on the back of Ryan's motorcycle.

Think about who always comes to your rescue when you need it the most.

"I really would prefer not to think about it," she said out loud. "Just this once."

Ryan gave her an odd look, but he was already revving up his little red machine. "Hop on, sweetheart," he told her. He zipped up his jacket and reached for his helmet. "Don't bother talking to me or arguing with me along the way, because I won't hear you, anyway."

With a rising feeling of anticipation, Lockett climbed onto the small area of leather seat left behind him, bunching up her skirts and feeling for the footrests.

There was no way around it, and no space for politeness. Her arms had to go around his hard, flat middle if she wanted to stay on the bike. Her front had to be plastered to his back unless she wanted to pitch right off over the fender.

Even if he dropped her off at the first bus stop, it promised to be a long, uncomfortable ride.

Lockett smiled.

This had nothing to do with running off into the sunset with Ryan, of course. Nothing had really changed between them—he was still impossible, still unpardonably connected to the mob, still a real bear when he wanted to be. And she was still looking for her dreams, and in no hurry to have the likes of Ryan pushing her around. He was an escape from a terrible wedding, and that was it.

But still... Although he didn't appear to be happy about this rescue, and she really hadn't decided how she felt, she couldn't deny that adventure returned to her life once Ryan sailed back into it. When they teamed up, *life* began to happen.

With her veil floating behind her, with sixteen yards of satin and lace blowing in the breeze, almost sideswiping the catering truck as it careered up the Kensington drive, they roared off into the sun.

"It appears there won't be a wedding today after all," Lockett said cheerfully. "Take that, Dad."

"WHERE ARE WE?" she asked, peering up at the most hilarious set of lights she had ever seen. It wasn't even dark yet, but the neon was blazing, outlining an almost naked, extremely curvy, pink woman clutching a fat red heart. It was positively lurid.

They had been driving forever, in circles it seemed, and her whole body was stiff from sitting on the motorcycle. Hanging on to Ryan had been no picnic, either.

Yeah, right. Like she hadn't rested her cheek on the smooth leather of his jacket and taken a nap there for a few minutes. Like she hadn't been fantasizing all sorts of outrageous things ever since they'd taken off. Like her body hadn't loved every minute of being wedged up against him like that, feeling the subtle play of his muscles as he shifted his weight, as he leaned into the turns, as her lace-covered thighs rubbed the heavy denim of his hard bottom.

Well, maybe her body thought it was great, but Lockett definitely did not. She didn't enjoy it in the least. She fanned her face with one hand.

"We're somewhere in Indiana," Ryan told her. He switched off the bike and began to unfold and stretch his long body. "Looks like a great place to stop, don't you think?"

"Well," she said dubiously, "I suppose so. But, Ryan..."

"Here it comes," he muttered. "Now she starts the objections."

"Well, it's called Honeymoon Haven," she protested. "That's what that big sign says. Honeymoon Haven. A Fantasy Resort For Lovers. Right next to the naked woman with the breast implants."

"I don't think they do breast implants in neon."

Lockett ignored him. "What's wrong with a nice hotel with a five-star French restaurant and a concierge? But a fantasy resort for *lovers?* Isn't that kind of awkward for the two of us?"

"Don't worry, Lockett." He gave her a wicked smile. "I promise to behave."

"I've heard of these kinds of motels," she said quickly. "Isn't this the kind of place where sleazy married men take their mistresses, where nerdlike people with odd fantasies go pretend to be cavemen or something?"

"And where women in wedding dresses show up in the lobby on a regular basis. Think about it, Lockett."

"There have to be other places we could go. How about Paris?" she asked wistfully. "Or Hawaii? There are plenty of brides there. We'll just drive back to O'Hare and get a nice flight somewhere."

With a resolute expression, Ryan pulled some kind of saddlebag off the motorcycle and started to back up across the parking lot toward the main building. "We don't have time for flights. By the time we got to Paris, Interpol would have our pictures and résumés. This is just far enough to be out of range, and close enough that we're not risking being seen. Another hour on the road and I bet there'd be helicopters searching for us."

"Helicopters? Don't you think you're overstating things a bit?"

"No," he said tersely. "I don't. We're staying here. At this kind of place, even if somebody does notice us, well, *not* noticing is part of their business."

"But nobody would've noticed us at your place, above the flower shop," she argued. "Why couldn't we go there?"

He regarded her shrewdly. "Don't you think that's the first place dear old dad would've looked?"

"He doesn't know where you live."

"Oh, yes, he does. He sent some of his pals to talk to me, remember?" he asked mockingly. "Besides, if Beatie can find me to send out the latest SOS, then your father shouldn't have any trouble."

"I really don't think..." She had been about to say that she really didn't think her father would bother to come after her. Once he got over the idea that his plans for the "merger" had been thwarted, surely he would be more reasonable.

But then she remembered the way he'd bellowed at her, and the angry color staining his face. This was no ordinary disappointment, no little tiff. For reasons she couldn't fathom, her father was vitally interested in marrying her off, and making it happen now. He *would* be coming after them, with all the weapons at his disposal.

His friends were congressmen and judges. He had plenty of weapons. And they were in deep trouble.

Oh, hell. She groaned. Ryan was starting to make sense to her. She was in worse shape than she thought.

Gathering up an armful of skirts, Lockett jumped off and went after him. "So what's the plan? What do we do now?"

"I don't know."

"You don't know?" she returned. "You mean, you don't have a plan?"

He shrugged. "I haven't exactly had time to think of one. I was just looking for someplace to lie low for the next couple of hours, to give us a chance to figure out our next move."

She let that sink in. "*Our* next move? So we are doing this together?"

Ryan didn't answer, just strode ever more quickly toward the Honeymoon Haven canopy. "That's something we'll have to talk about. We don't even know what we're doing yet, let alone who we're doing it with."

"Okay. I guess that's reasonable. How bad can it be?" she asked out loud, gazing up at the garish pink-and-red striped canopy. "At least it's...different."

But the lobby of this Honeymoon Haven was much stranger than she'd expected. Aside from a profusion of hearts and flowers, and a red velvet decor that hurt her eyes, there were three huge pink-marble fountains, topped by pairs of equally pink cupids spouting pink-dyed water from their chubby little mouths. Doves had been suspended in the air as an added attraction.

It made the lobby look vaguely like a giant Valentine Day birdbath. Bizarre, indeed.

Lockett took it all in with wide eyes. She had never seen anything this ostentatiously tacky in her entire life.

"Oh, my," she whispered to Ryan as he approached the front desk where a young lady in a red baby-doll smock waited to serve them. "Do you think all this plastic and polyester is healthy?"

"You'll love it, Lockett. Trust me."

"Hi," the girl behind the counter offered. "Nice dress. Came right from the wedding, huh? Cool. We get a lot of those. You know, brides who don't want to pop for the going away outfit. Or maybe they just want to get some more mileage out of the wedding gown. Not much you can do with them after the big day, huh?"

"Do I look like the sort of person who would need to get mileage out of her wedding gown?" Lockett muttered. She stopped when she realized that at this moment in time, after being buffeted about by wind and road dust, she probably looked very much like a bride on a budget. Her veil had blown off somewhere near the Illinois-Indiana border, and her hair probably looked like it had been through a world war. Not exactly the perfect bride. She set her jaw and shut her mouth.

"Let me guess," the clerk mused, scanning Ryan and his leather attire up and down. "You're going into our Motorcycle Mama suite."

"No," Lockett answered gaily. "No motorcycle mamas here."

"Oh, shoot. I'm usually so good at guessing." The girl frowned, glancing back and forth between them. "Did you reserve Count Dracula's Castle of Love? Maybe the Starship Erotica? I would've said Parisian Paradise, with the see-through champagne glass hot tub—that's a biggie for newlyweds—but I know somebody's been in it for the past two weeks."

"Someone's been in the hot tub for the past two weeks?" Lockett asked in horror.

"No, in the Parisian Paradise suite." She giggled. "So what did you reserve?"

"Actually, we don't have a reservation." Ryan slid a fifty-dollar bill across the counter. Lockett eyed it dubiously. Could he afford a fifty-dollar tip? Cash seemed like a precious commodity at the moment, since she didn't have any. But the desk clerk snapped up the money without batting an eye.

Ryan continued. "We forgot to make a reservation. Do you have anything available?"

"Oh, wow, we're like, packed. We have a waiting list a mile long for just about everything." She chewed her lip. "But I hate to see you sleep in the parking lot on your wedding night."

"Exactly," Ryan said with an ingratiating smile. He reached over and gave his pseudobride a squeeze, as if to telegraph how anxious they were to be alone. Lockett managed a thin smile. This whole charade made her want to throw up. As if she hadn't already had enough of the wedding business to last her a lifetime.

"Let me see what we've got." The girl in red seemed to search various lists, finally turning back to them. "Okay, here's what I can do. Dungeon o' Desire is open. Or I have Ride 'Em Cowboy. That's usually real popular, but we had somebody push back their reservation a day. So if it's for one night only, I can give you Ride 'Em Cowboy."

"'Ride 'Em Cowboy'?" Lockett echoed doubtfully.

"It's really cute. You'll love it," the clerk promised.

"It's either that or the Dungeon o' Desire," Ryan noted. "It's your call."

"Well, it has to be better than a dungeon." Lockett shuddered. "I don't handle cold and creepy well."

"It's kind of different, that's for sure." The clerk said.

Lockett couldn't believe she was in this place.

"So I guess Ride 'Em Cowboy it is." The girl pushed a register around for Ryan to sign. After reading what he wrote and running off a credit card, she said, "Here's your key, Mr. Haven."

"Mr. Haven?" Lockett whispered, but he gave her a quelling stare.

"Be quiet, *Mrs.* Haven."

"Aha," she said. "Honeymoon Haven. Mr. and Mrs. Haven. I get it!"

Ryan gave her a swift elbow.

Meanwhile the clerk rattled on with what sounded like a prerecorded speech, oblivious to any suspicious behavior by her guests. Maybe Ryan was right; maybe it was their business not to notice.

"You'll need to go through this building and out into Lover's Lagoon," she instructed them. "Lover's Lagoon is kind of the center of everything here, and the other buildings go around it, like spokes on a wheel. Get it? Okay, so you should follow the trail of blue tiki torches until you see a bridge marked All-American Amour—that's where our suites on the American theme are. Ride 'Em Cowboy is the second suite on your left, right after Indian Love Call. If you hit Fairytale Forest, you've gone too far."

"'Fairytale Forest'?" Lockett repeated weakly. What with cowboys and Indians, not to mention dungeons and Dracula, she was beginning to feel light-headed.

"Come along, Mrs. Haven," Ryan said sardonically. "Lover's Lagoon awaits us."

"Which reminds me, Mr. Haven." She lowered her voice. "You gave her a credit card. Don't you think she'll notice the names don't match? Won't whoever is coming after us be able to trace you through your credit cards?"

"My name's not on the card. It's untraceable."

Who had ever heard of a credit card with no name on it? Well, maybe a corporate card... But what would Ryan be doing with one? With his long hair and black leather wardrobe, she couldn't imagine any corporation he'd be associated with.

Unless it was something to do with Uncle Max.

The whole thing struck her as extremely suspicious. Under normal circumstances, she had enough integrity to refuse to live off dirty money and credit cards. But at the moment she didn't have a whole lot of choices. It was either sticking with Ryan or hitchhiking on the freeway in her wedding dress. She didn't have a toothbrush, let alone a wallet. So she didn't force the issue, or ask questions, and she didn't get answers she really didn't want to hear. It was really a good deal.

"Well, what do you know? Lover's Lagoon is the swimming pool. Want to go for a dip later if we can find you something to wear?" he asked in an annoyingly normal voice.

Her whole life was falling apart, and he wanted to go for a dip in a plastic pool. "I think you're actually enjoying this. Are you insane?"

He caught her hand and dragged her along behind him. "Lighten up, Lockett. Have some fun. How often do you get to see a place as crazy as this?"

"Well, I was hoping for never," she said brightly, "but I guess I'll have to settle."

He shook his head. "Same old Lockett."

He strode on ahead, following a line of bright blue tiki torches around the edge of the elaborate pool area. Jungle vines and thick greenery separated levels of small waterfalls and tide pools where scantily clad couples splashed and swam. There were plenty of nooks and crannies for illicit lovers with water games in mind, as well as a larger area where more open folk could play. In the background a soundtrack of jungle noises provided chirps and birdcalls, with a sort of Tarzan-in-the-Amazon feel.

She couldn't help herself. She was too tired to hold back. "This is amazing."

"So you're starting to like it?"

"Like it? I think it's disgusting!"

"You always did start to whine the minute the silver spoon slipped out of your mouth," he groused.

"This has nothing to do with money," she scoffed, stumbling over a particularly hideous plastic monkey that decorated the trail. "It has to do with all these people carrying on illicit affairs here, underneath the plastic palm trees."

"Same old Lockett."

He held out a hand to help her across the rope bridge that led out of Lover's Lagoon and on to the next disaster area, but Lockett swatted him away. She preferred to traverse rope bridges in heels all by herself, even if it meant lurching a bit.

"Here's another thing." She pointed to the sign indicating the new building they were entering. "It's called All-American Amour. Now what sense does that make? All-American, and the next word is in French."

But he was already stopping in front of a door, fitting the key into the lock of the Ride 'Em Cowboy suite. "Same old Lockett," he muttered again.

Couldn't he think of anything else to say? "Same old Lockett" was really starting to get on her nerves. In the old days she would've backed off from a fight with him. But today she was just tired enough—and plenty cranky—to give back as good as she got.

"I hate it when you say things like that," she told him. "You get that superior tone in your voice, like you think you're Abe Lincoln, Man of the People, or something."

If he'd heard her, he gave no indication. But he did let out a low whistle as he swung open the door. "I guess I should say 'Yee-haw.'"

Lockett brought up the rear. Another chapter in the surreal saga of Honeymoon Haven awaited. The Ride 'Em Cowboy suite had two levels—a long oval that formed the main area, and a bedroom part that went up a few steps back to the right.

None of that was anything extraordinary. What was fantastic was the way it had been decorated.

The wall to the left was painted to look like a desert sunset, and there was a large, round sunken tub flush up against it. A small hand-lettered sign proclaimed it to be The Watering Hole. The faucets and the towel bars were shaped like cacti. She supposed it was the bathtub for the room, but it was right out in the open, with no walls or protection. Breezy bathing built for two, it appeared.

The wall on the right was done in some sort of wanted-poster wallpaper, and it was outfitted as if it were in a stable. At least, that was Lockett's best guess. There were lots of rusty-looking hooks, from which hung chaps, riding crops, a gun belt and requisite six-shooters, a bull whip, a saddle, even what appeared to be pieces of clothing, as if a saloon girl had dropped off

her feather boa and her knickers in her flight out of the
O.K. Corral.

Lockett couldn't stop gaping. "Look at that junk,"
she managed. "Somebody went to a lot of trouble
finding all those things just for decoration."

"Decoration?" Ryan raised an eyebrow. "I, uh,
think that would be up to the individual."

"What would?"

"What you use it for."

"You mean, people use those things?" She stared at
him, openmouthed. "For what?"

"Do I have to fill in the blanks?"

Her gaze wandered over the chaps and the corset.
Okay, maybe some hardy souls got into playing dress-
up. But what about the gun belt? And the saddle?
"You're making this up."

He shrugged again.

"I d-don't believe you," she sputtered. "Not the
saddle."

There was a pause. "Why do you think they call it
Ride 'Em Cowboy?"

"The *saddle?*" Her voice rose about an octave. She
was outraged. "How do you—"

"How do *they* use the saddle?" He gave her a small
smile, and his knowing gaze held her steadily. "Well, I
think one person would wear it and the other person
would, uh, do the riding—"

"That's not what I meant!" Lockett felt her cheeks
flush with rosy color. She had never been so embarrassed in her life. "What have you been doing that you
know about this kind of thing?"

His eyes never left her. "I have a good imagination."

"There's nothing good about your imagination," she muttered. But she couldn't stop thinking about that saddle. People just didn't do that sort of thing. At least, not people in her circle of acquaintance.

Once again he had made it very apparent that they were as different as day and night.

Meanwhile, Ryan wandered off to check out the rest of the place. "There's a bar over here," he said, switching on a red lantern attached to the front wall and illuminating the long, dark bar back there. It looked like it was fully stocked with Old Red Eye and sarsaparilla. Immediately the huge, nude oil painting that hung behind the bar also came into focus.

Lockett already thought the Western theme was overdone, without that corpulent nude. She sat down on a red velvet chaise longue near the wanted-poster wall and started to remove her shoes and stockings. She couldn't wait to wiggle her toes.

"Are you hungry?" Ryan inquired. "Thirsty? There's a small refrigerator back here."

"Whiskey, neat," she announced, and then she laughed when she caught the look on his face. "I suppose I should eat something. I haven't had anything all day, at least not that I can remember."

"Quite a day."

"I'll say. Your wedding day is supposed to be memorable, but not like this." She sighed and closed her eyes, leaning back into the settee. "I wish I'd had a chance to see the food for the reception. It was supposed to be pretty wonderful, little crepes and crab puffs and things..." Her stomach growled under its layers of satin and lace. "And I had to leave my cake behind," she said sadly.

"Missing the cake is the least of your worries."

"I know." She opened her eyes. Ryan looked pensive as he stood behind the big bar. "Thank you, by the way. I don't know what rescue we're up to. This is getting ridiculous."

"I know."

Lockett shook her head. She wished she had a really good hairbrush. She wished she had a white cotton nightgown, her favorite silk robe, a big glass of Coke on ice, and an even bigger box of Frango mints.

She wished she could go back and fix everything.

"I still don't know how this happened," she whispered. "One minute my life was absolutely perfect, and the next, my fiancé is behaving as if he's had a lobotomy, and my father is acting like a raving lunatic. Suddenly my life is in ashes. I'm on the lam like a common criminal. I'm stuck in the strangest motel this side of the Marquis de Sade's Wayside Inn. And all because—"

"Because you spent the night with me," he finished for her. His expression was cool and unreadable.

"I was going to say it was because I got cold feet about getting married," she said lightly. "But I suppose your way is as good as mine."

Ryan skirted out from behind the bar and handed her a can of Coke and a candy bar. "So what's next?"

She just stared down at the soda and the chocolate. Was he reading her mind?

"The immediate rescue is out of the way," Ryan noted. "Beatie made me promise to get you out of the house and away from your father, and I did that. So what do you want to do next, Lockett?"

"I have no idea." She glanced down at her gown. "Aside from finding something else to wear. You don't suppose these rooms come stocked with robes, do you?"

"I doubt it." After a quick glance at the facilities, Ryan moved to the closet, where he began to poke around. "We've got a couple of pairs of cowboy boots and some kind of dress thing that looks like it's left-over from a road company of *Best Little Whorehouse in Texas*." He held up a skimpy slice of red polyester with a few feathers attached. "Are you game for that?"

"Heavens, no!" she protested. Not that she would wear polyester anyway, but... "You have no idea where those things have been."

"I'm sure they're laundered in between guests. It's no different from the robes in the closets at the Ritz."

"I don't care." She huddled in her wedding dress, wishing vainly she were at the Ritz. Anywhere you could call for the concierge to bring you a new outfit from the nearest Christian Dior boutique and charge it to your room. Anywhere where her choices were better than cowboy boots and Whore of Babylon outfits. A hysterical giggle escaped her. "Whore of Babylon would be in some other suite. This one has Whore of Dodge City."

"What did you say?"

"Nothing." She raised her chin. "I couldn't possibly wear that thing."

Ryan sighed, but he didn't say anything. His feelings about her impossibly high standards were already clear. "Do you want me to go out and find you something else?"

"Yes, thank you," she said primly. "Maybe there's a gift shop in this place. Maybe you could find me some sort of basic outfit. Something in cotton or silk. No polyester."

He sighed again. "Lockett... How likely is it that a gift shop at the Honeymoon Haven would have anything in silk?"

"You could at least try. You won't know until you do," she said stubbornly.

"All right. I suppose." But there was a less agreeable tone to his voice when he added, "You really are a royal pain, Lockett. Anybody else would be glad to find safe harbor. But you're complaining about polyester and whether the saloon girl outfit in the closet has a designer label."

"I didn't say—"

But he turned away. "Just forget it. Some things never change, that's all. You always were a spoiled little princess and you still are."

"If I'm so spoiled and so impossible, then why do you keep rescuing me?"

But all she heard was the slam of the front door to the Ride 'Em Cowboy suite. Ryan had already left, venturing out in search of haute couture for his haughty bride.

Chapter Eight

Slippery Saddles

He took a sort of perverse pleasure in the outfit he found for her. He smiled. Lockett was going to hate it.

It wasn't his fault, of course. The gift shop didn't have anything she would've remotely liked. So he picked something he knew would infuriate her, and he even read the tag to be sure. One hundred percent polyester. Perfect.

And then, because he really was a decent guy, he threw in shampoo and a hairbrush. But as he ambled back to their suite, picking his way back through Lover's Lagoon, he pondered the situation between them.

Had her pretentious attitude gotten worse over the years, or was it just his imagination? Was the Lockett he remembered, who was smart and funny and eager to experience life in all its diversity, hiding in there somewhere? Or was he fooling himself?

So far, she was doing a great imitation of being a real hoity-toity, bred-in-the-bone, don't-soil-the-hem-of-my-gown snob.

Funny, he had always accused her of being a bit too high-and-mighty, but he'd really thought, deep down, it was more of a habit than an integral part of her personality. He'd even understood when she'd had difficulty adjusting to life in the poor lane, when she and their short-lived marriage had started to show signs of strain.

Even from the beginning he had feared that the reckoning would come sooner or later.

After all, how could he have expected someone like Lockett Kensington to go for life in a fifth-floor walkup. Hope, maybe, but not really believe. Back then, his meager finances couldn't come near to providing the kind of life she was used to. Hell, he couldn't even have provided the kind of life her *servants* were used to.

So when things had gotten more and more tense, when she'd finally just cut out completely, he couldn't say he was surprised. At the time, it had almost been a relief when the other shoe had dropped and she'd finally cleared out and gone back home to Daddy.

An agonizing, burning stab in the heart, but a relief, too.

Just like when she'd bolted from his apartment this morning. Another stab right to the heart. Another relief.

Was that only this morning? It already felt like weeks since he'd held her and touched her...since he'd peeled her dress off and tucked her into his bed.

He clenched his jaw. All the old passion was definitely there.

But so were all the old problems. They jumped up and bit him on the nose the moment he looked at her. And now that he'd rescued her again, it made the situation that much more impossible.

He leaned against the wall outside the suite for just a second, not anxious to go in and start Round Three of the bantamweight boxing championship.

Why was he here? And why was she? What was it that kept throwing them together when they so clearly didn't belong?

Even in the midst of this mental torture, Ryan smiled to himself. He couldn't help it. He remembered popping up over the windowsill and seeing the look on her face. It was such fun to shock her, to push her, to see how far she would go before she pushed back.

But his smile faded. When he'd vaulted in her window, he saw the most beautiful bride he could've ever imagined. Against all that white lace, Lockett positively glowed. In that fabulous dress, with the veil and the jewelry and the sparkle in her eyes, she took his breath away.

That was the picture she was meant to make on her wedding day.

He remembered their wedding, if you could even call it that. He remembered standing up in front of some shabby justice of the peace in a town he had long since forgotten the name of, mumbling about three words, and then hightailing it right out of there.

Instead of a beautiful white gown, Lockett had worn jeans and a cheap sweater they'd picked up along the way. He'd felt even then that their rushed vows were desperately inadequate to show her how much he loved her, how happy he was to have won the hand of a princess.

He should've known it would never last.

Behind him, the door to the suite swung inward with a whoosh.

"What are you doing out there?" Lockett asked. "I was beginning to think you were never coming back."

"I always come back." He edged past her, flapping his gift shop bag against his thigh. "Or hadn't you noticed?"

"I noticed. I—I was just getting worried, that's all." Quietly she shut the door behind him. "It's kind of frightening to be sitting here all by yourself in a dress you can't get out of, wondering what's going to happen to you. I mean, what would I do if you didn't come back?" Her face was pale and her blue eyes were wide and anxious. "I don't have a dime to my name. I don't have anywhere else to go."

What was this he saw? Cracks of vulnerability in Miss Lockett Kensington's impervious facade?

"Lucky for you you've got a stooge who always rescues you in the nick of time," he said sardonically. He tossed the bag down on the settee. "A new wardrobe, as ordered, ma'am."

She and her dress swept along behind him. She picked up the bag, but she didn't open it, just twisted and retwisted the top edge. "Okay, fine, but first I think we really need to settle some things."

"Don't you even want to see what I brought you?" He gave her a measuring glance. "I thought you were in such a hurry to get out of that dress."

"Well, I was, but I've had some time to think while you were gone."

"Always a dangerous proposition," he said dryly.

"Don't make fun of me, Ryan! I'm not in the mood." She dropped the bag back on the settee and spun away from him. With her wide skirts crashing along like the wake of a luxury liner, she paced back and forth. "I don't know why you're here, or what you want from me. I don't understand why you keep jumping back into my life when you so clearly dislike me."

"I never said I—"

"It's pretty obvious, Ryan." She frowned at him. "What's in this for you?"

"Nothing, as far as I know."

"Do you want money? Is that it?" she asked quickly. "But I don't have any. And getting access to any of my bank accounts would alert my father immediately."

He felt as if he'd been slapped. "I don't want your money," he said in a soft, dangerous voice.

"All right. But I still don't get it."

He wondered whether she could hear the anger in his voice. He wondered if she knew how completely she had managed to insult him. "Does it matter why I do what I do?"

"Yes," she persisted. "It matters to me. I want to have this all figured out."

"We can talk about that later." His gaze slashed up and down her body in a purposely contemptuous manner. "First I want you to get out that idiotic dress. I'm really sick of looking at it. I think you'd better go up to the bedroom and change right now."

She flushed with anger. "Sorry." With dignity, she reached for the bag from the gift shop and then started up the steps to the bedroom area. "But when I come back, we are going to get this settled."

Smartly, she opened the door and let herself into the bedroom. She had gone no more than three steps when she let out a shriek of absolute horror.

He was there in a flash. "What is it?"

"That," she responded, clutching his arm and pointing to the center of the room.

It was a stagecoach. Or rather, a bed fitted out to look like a stagecoach. There were no doors on it, so you could see the mattress and the pillows inside. But otherwise, it was a perfect model of a stagecoach, wheels and luggage racks and everything, right out of all those old movies where the guys in the black hats came hooting and hollering down to rob the passengers.

"Why are you scared of a stagecoach?"

"What is it doing here?"

"It's the bed, Lockett. See the pillows inside?" He drew her over closer. "It's just a bed. Why didn't you notice it before this?"

"I don't know. I was just sitting there in the main room, eating my candy bar, waiting for you." She peered inside the bed. "I hadn't had a chance to look around yet."

"So they gave us a goofy bed that fits the theme. No big deal."

"It's pretty small," she said apprehensively, circling it, examining the wobbly stairs that led up to the side opening. "Not meant for anyone with claustrophobia."

"I doubt they were worried about that when they built it," he noted.

"Where are you going to sleep?"

"In the stagecoach," he told her flatly. "I'm not the one with the problem about it."

"But then where will I—"

"In the stagecoach," he repeated. "There's no place else. We're adults. We can handle it."

She sent him a doubtful look, but she didn't say anything. Instead she very carefully eased open the next door, the only one they hadn't looked in yet, as if she expected something or someone in there to bite her.

"Not too bad," she said with relief. "It's woody in here, but it seems okay, just a big barrel around the shower, with some kind of ugly snake for a shower head. And then a perfectly normal toilet. I guess there's nothing they can do to a toilet."

"If there was, I'm sure they would've done it."

"Right."

"So are you okay now? Are you going to change your clothes?"

"I can hardly change my clothes in a stagecoach," she protested. "It's not the same as a regular old bed where you can sit while you take things off. Besides, I can't get out of this thing by myself. You'll have to help me. So we have to go back down to the chaise."

And out she trooped, leaving the stagecoach up there all by itself. Ryan trailed after her, suddenly wondering about all this.

Standing over by the watering hole, Lockett lifted her hair and presented the back of her neck. "Here. The buttons start there."

"Okay, I've got it."

But it wasn't okay. It was much too close and much too tempting. Even after a few hours on the back of his bike, Lockett's neck still smelled of expensive soap and sweet perfume. A tendril of fine golden hair twined around the first button and he had to gently disentangle it to get to the button. Her hair felt so silky between his fingers, and her skin was so smooth when his thumb barely brushed it.

Lockett went very still.

He had the maddening urge to bend down and press his lips to the warm curve of her nape, *there*, where she held her hair out of the way, where her skin was as bare and as soft as a summer peach.

It wouldn't take much. And he knew, as well as he did about anything, how quickly, and easily, Lockett would respond.

He knew that as soon as his tongue touched her neck, she would sigh and moan and drift backward into his embrace. He knew his hands would come up around her, cupping her breasts through the lace and satin, fingering her, stroking her, driving her insane, until she turned to him, kissing him, begging him....

And then they'd tumble to the floor, making love as crazy and as wild as they had when they were too young to know any better.

Oh, God, this was torture. He hadn't so much as touched her yet, and already he was aching with the need to be with her completely.

He held himself rigid. He forced his body back under control.

Antonio Ryan had never been a slave to his passions, and he had no intention of giving in now. Fiercely, he reined himself in.

Keeping a certain distance between them, he reached for the first button. Delicately, ever so slowly, his long fingers worked to push the tiny pearl through its lacy loop. So small. So fragile. So impossible.

He felt ham-handed, huge, clumsy. He felt like he had no right to touch anything so fine.

"Look, I can't do this." He backed away. "I'm sorry, but I can't—"

"Are the buttons too small?" she asked, twirling around to look him in the eye. "Too many?"

Her face was flushed and rosy, her mouth parted slightly, as if she were having trouble breathing, and her eyes were alive with fire and heat.

She read my mind, he thought suddenly. *She's as turned on as I am.*

"If you can't get the buttons, then just rip it," she said recklessly. "Just rip it. What good is it to me, anyway? I don't care if it turns into a pile of rags. I have to get out of this thing."

Ryan hesitated.

Her voice was husky, seething, as she said again, *"Rip it!"*

And so he did. He took one hand, he grabbed the top of her dress, and he tore down angrily, scattering pearl buttons every which way, rending the fabric, baring Lockett's back to the waist.

One more second and he would've had his hands inside what was left of her wedding gown. He would've had her in his arms, plastered up against him, and neither one of them would have stood a chance.

But Lockett whirled away, clutching the dress together in front, scooping up the bag and heading up to the bedroom.

"Lockett, I—" he began. He didn't know what he was going to say. Apologize for losing his cool? Blame her for starting the whole thing?

But she shut the door. And then, oddly enough, he heard the distinct sound of her laughter.

"Ryan, is this your idea of a joke?" she called out.

It came back to him. He recalled now what he had bought her to wear. Even in the haze of his leftover passion, he managed a smile. He couldn't wait to see her in it.

But she made him wait.

He heard rustling around up there, a slam or bang or two, and then the rush of the shower. Finally, after he'd put up his feet and pulled off his boots, after he'd cooled off for several long minutes, Lockett poked her head around the door at the top of the stairs. Her hair was wet, but neatly combed, and she looked very apprehensive.

"This is truly ridiculous," she mumbled.

He grinned at her. "Aw, come on. It was the best I could find."

Very tentatively, she stuck one foot out on the steps. "The least you can do is look away, so I don't feel like some kind of sleazebucket Miss America contestant or something, romping down the stairs in a bathing suit."

"It's a not a bathing suit."

"I wish it were," she murmured. "It would probably cover more."

"Come on. You were so hot to talk, to settle things." He leaned back on the settee, bracing his head on folded arms, but his eyes never left her. "We can't do that with you up there and me down here."

With a pained expression, Lockett slowly left the protection of the door. Ryan had the urge to whistle. Or maybe sit up and beg.

He stayed where he was. What had he thought he was doing, buying her that? How was he going to keep his hands off her when she was wearing that thing? This was supposed to be a little joke to tweak her pretensions. Instead it had turned into a major test of his self-control. So far, he was losing. Big time.

The outfit was black and skimpy, and it looked a hell of a lot better on her than in the gift shop. He had thought it was supposed to be some kind of short set, although on Lockett's long, spectacular legs, it didn't

come down far enough to be anything but underwear.
The pants were tight, a second skin, and he knew there
would be a see-through handprint on the curve of one
round little cheek when she turned around.

Right now, she had her own hand back there as she
tiptoed down the stairs, so he figured she was covering
it up.

And then there was the top. On the hanger, it had
seemed like a normal enough T-shirt, with some more
of those sheer handprints decorating the front. But on
Lockett the handprints lined up in exactly the right
places to create complete havoc. The fingers dipped
down over her breasts, as if the guy with the hands was
getting ready to grab her. As she descended, the fingers
slithered over her curves, and her breasts bobbed gently against the slinky fabric.

Ryan stifled a groan, but he felt it echo deep inside.
His hands itched to match up with those handprints. He
smashed them inside his jeans' pockets before they did
any wandering, and he frowned darkly, staring at a hole
in the floor.

There was no way he was going to be able to talk to
her like that without losing his mind. There was no way
he'd be able to coexist in the same hemisphere with her
in that without losing control.

"Here," he said, rummaging in his saddlebag until he
found an extra T-shirt. "Put this on over it."

"Oh, thank you," she whispered. "There aren't any
mirrors up there, so I can only imagine how horrible I
look."

Horrible? *Not a chance, sweetheart.* But too sultry
for her own good. And way too steamy for his peace of
mind.

She yanked the T-shirt down over her head so fast he almost missed the flash of creamy skin at her waist where her top gapped above her pants. Almost, but not quite.

And then she stood there, opposite him, with his T-shirt down to her knees, chewing her lip.

"Well?" he prompted. A whole ten seconds had elapsed and he thought he was doing pretty good not to have tossed her on the floor and thrown away the T-shirt by now. "What did you want to tell me?"

She hesitated. Finally she ventured, "I'm going to come over there and sit down, too, okay? I'm sorry, but the chaise is the only piece of furniture in here unless you want to go up and hop in the stagecoach, so I have to sit next to you."

"Okay," he agreed. He edged over to make room for her.

"But you have to promise not to touch me," she said carefully. "Weird things happen when you touch me, and I really don't want to deal with that right now."

She didn't have to convince him. The throbbing ache in his loins was proof enough that she was right.

"Come on. Sit down already," he said, grumbling. "I won't come near you."

After a moment Lockett consented to perch on the end of the red velvet settee, staring straight ahead into the cowboy sunset on the far wall.

"Well, Ryan," she began in a funny, cool little voice. "I did some thinking while you were out on your shopping spree, and some more while I was in the shower. As I see it, we've made it this far. Step one—to escape from the wedding—accomplished."

"Right."

"So here's my first question," she went on, still gazing at the painted sunset. "I know this really had nothing to do with you, and there's no reason you shouldn't just dump me and go back to your regular life. But I hope you're willing to stick around long enough to help me find some way out of this mess. Are you?"

"I don't really think I have a choice."

That got her attention. Shifting to face him, she asked, "I already told you I can't pay you anything. So you could easily decide this isn't worth it, and you're out of it. I mean, I wouldn't blame you. None of this is your problem."

"It's been my problem ever since your father's goon paid me a visit to tell me to stay away from you." Ryan knew his expression was forbidding, but he didn't care. She'd brought up that crap about paying him again, and it made him so damn mad he couldn't see straight. "As you can tell, I didn't obey the instructions. In fact, I snatched you right out from under their noses—twice. I think your daddy has just as much of a score to settle with me as he does with you."

"Oh." Lockett swallowed. "I hadn't really thought of it that way."

But Ryan continued. "So I can't go back. Not until we know why he needs to marry you off to Stanford Marsh, and how to stop whatever it is he has in the works, once and for all."

"But that's just what I thought," Lockett said quickly. She scooted over closer, and fixed him with an eager, earnest gaze. "First, I was thinking we should just wait things out, and see what happens once the fuss over the canceled wedding dies down. It's possible that my father's a little peeved because I didn't obey him, but there's no major schism here. So under that plan, I could just hide out for a while, and once things cool off, I go home."

"Lockett, I really don't—"

"No, wait, because I know what you're going to say. The chances of that happening are remote." She nodded. "I agree. I know my father. This is no minor disagreement. His pride is on the line. I'll bet he tells people I have the flu or something, and then he tries to find me as quickly as possible and get the wedding back on track."

"I'll buy that."

"So we have to do a little sleuthing, before he locates me, and we figure out what's behind all this." She was on a roll now. "I mean, there has to be something going on that I don't know about, something that made my marrying Stanford absolutely critical for some reason. I think that if we work together, we can get to the bottom of it."

"What if this turns out to be more than just a family tiff? What if there's something more involved? Like something illegal?" he asked. "We have to consider that possibility. Are you ready to expose your high-and-mighty old man, no matter how much of a stain it puts on him and the Kensington family name?"

"I don't know." Softly she whispered, "Considering the fact that he threatened to lock me in my room until I married Stanford, you'd think I'd be willing to throw him away, too." She shook her head. "But I just don't know. And I may not have to face that. I mean, it may be a business deal, and he may be going a bit too far, but I really doubt it's anything illegal. That's just not like my father at all."

"Wake up and smell the roses."

"Oh, come on, Ryan. You have no better idea than I do of what's behind this." She stood and stared him down. "You're hoping it will be something really seamy just to stick it to my dad because he stands for everything you hate—wealth, power, position, whatever. Okay, so he's not a great human being. But he's no crook. That kind of thing just doesn't happen in *my* family."

Ryan had his suspicions that that's exactly what her father was. But he knew she'd never believe him, not unless it was staring her in the face.

But he rose to his feet, as well. With both of them barefoot, he towered over her. "Was that crack supposed to refer to my uncle? Your father's no crook, but my family is, is that it?"

"Well, actually, no, I wasn't thinking about Max, but since you brought it up..." Lockett pressed her lips together and retreated a step. "Look, this is getting us nowhere. What do you say we call a truce? If we're going to work together and stay in this ridiculous place, we can't be squabbling all the time."

"A truce?" He crossed his arms over his chest. "Okay. Let's hear what that means to you, princess. Shoot."

Lockett lifted her chin. She crossed her arms, too, as if to show him she could be every bit as tough as he could. Even wearing his T-shirt, with wet hair, and a painted sunset for a backdrop, her demeanor was regal, uncompromising.

"It means," she announced, "that you will call me neither a princess nor a spoiled brat, and you will never again refer to silver spoons in my presence."

"And?"

"And I will, in return, refrain from mentioning Uncle Max or your financial situation, no matter how dire it may be . . ."

If she only knew. He gave her a hint of a smile. "Go on."

She turned away, and her voice grew a bit more indistinct. "And I will never say a word about what happened when our marriage broke up."

That was a bolt from the blue. They had never specifically talked about it before, even though they'd always managed to come back to the issues in dispute—her money, his lack of it. They'd even talked about what had happened after, and why he hadn't gone to school. But she'd already covered that. "What do you mean?" he asked softly. "What do you mean, what happened?"

Lockett dug a toe into the rug. "I mean, how it all fell out—the ugly stuff."

He still had no idea what she was talking about. "What ugly stuff?"

"Okay," she conceded, wheeling back to him, hugging herself tightly over the borrowed T-shirt. "If you want me to spell it out for you, I will. I promise, as part of our truce, never to bring up the fact that you offered to divorce me for a lousy half a million bucks."

"I offered to *what?*" he shouted.

"Okay, so maybe it was an annulment and not a divorce. I didn't read it that closely. What, didn't you know I knew? Did you think it was still a secret?"

He grabbed her by the shoulders. Very carefully, he asked, "Why did you think I wanted to divorce you for a million dollars?"

"Half a million," she responded softly.

NO COST! NO OBLIGATION TO BUY!
NO PURCHASE NECESSARY!

PLAY "LUCKY 7" AND GET FIVE FREE GIFTS

HOW TO PLAY:

1. With a coin, carefully scratch off the silver box at the right. Then check the claim chart to see what we have for you—FREE BOOKS and a gift—ALL YOURS! ALL FREE!

2. Send back this card and you'll receive brand-new Harlequin American Romance® novels. These books have a cover price of $3.50 each, but they are yours to keep absolutely free.

3. There's no catch. You're under no obligation to buy anything. We charge nothing—ZERO—for your first shipment. And you don't have to make any minimum number of purchases—not even one!

4. The fact is thousands of readers enjoy receiving books by mail from the Harlequin Reader Service®. They like the convenience of home delivery...they like getting the best new novels months before they're available in stores...and they love our discount prices!

5. We hope that after receiving your free books you'll want to remain a subscriber. But the choice is yours—to continue or cancel, anytime at all! So why not take us up on our invitation, with no risk of any kind. You'll be glad you did!

You'll love this plush, cuddly Teddy Bear, an adorable accessory for your dressing table, bookcase or desk. Measuring 5½" tall, he's soft and brown and has a bright red ribbon around his neck—he's completely captivating! And he's yours *absolutely free*, when you accept this no-risk offer!

Just scratch off the silver box with a coin. Then check below to see the gifts you get.

YES! I have scratched off the silver box. Please send me all the gifts for which I qualify. I understand I am under no obligation to purchase any books, as explained on the back and on the opposite page.

154 CIH ASYN
(U-H-AR-03/95)

NAME

ADDRESS   APT.

CITY   STATE   ZIP

7	7	7	WORTH FOUR FREE BOOKS PLUS A FREE CUDDLY TEDDY BEAR
🍒	🍒	🍒	WORTH THREE FREE BOOKS
●	●	●	WORTH TWO FREE BOOKS
🔔	🔔	🍒	WORTH ONE FREE BOOK

THE HARLEQUIN READER SERVICE®: HERE'S HOW IT WORKS

Accepting free books places you under no obligation to buy anything. You may keep the books and gift and return the shipping statement marked "cancel". If you do not cancel, about a month later we'll send you 4 additional novels, and bill you just $2.89 each plus 25¢ delivery and applicable sales tax, if any.* That's the complete price, and—compared to cover prices of $3.50 each—quite a bargain! You may cancel at any time, but if you choose to continue, every month we'll send you 4 more books, which you may either purchase at the discount price…or return at our expense and cancel your subscription.

*Terms and prices subject to change without notice. Sales tax applicable in N.Y.

Holding her immobile, staring down at her, Ryan could see the hurt in her eyes. Remembered hurt? Or was this still a fresh wound, after all these years? Silently he cursed her for ever believing such nonsense, at the same time he cursed himself for never knowing, not even having a clue, that this was why she'd left.

"But, Lockett, I obviously never got any money. How could that story be true?"

"You didn't get it because *I* left you," she reasoned. "Once I found out you were trying to extort money from my father, I went home. There was no need to pay you off."

"Extort money from your father? Does that sound like something I would do?" He didn't know whether to be angrier that she believed him capable of extortion, or that she thought his feelings were so shallow he would sell her out for a pile of cash.

"No, it didn't sound like you." Her eyes were wide and blue. "But he had the proof, Ryan. He showed it to me."

"What kind of proof?" he demanded.

"Does it really matter?" She shook off his hands, rubbing her arms and staring away at nothing. "I didn't want to believe it. I loved you. But things were already bad between us by then. You were so moody all the time. Nothing I did was right. I knew you were unhappy—"

"You were the unhappy one."

"Okay, so we were both miserable." She released an aggravated sigh. "This is exactly the conversation I was trying to avoid. I wanted to call a truce, remember? I was hoping we wouldn't have to dredge this stuff up anymore. It's water under the bridge."

Her gaze met his, and he knew that she was trying to pretend it didn't matter anymore. Hell, it mattered to him. These accusations were brand-new as far as he was concerned. He would have liked a chance to defend himself.

"If we're going to work together," she went on in that same level, unaffected tone, "we have to have some ground rules. We will avoid certain subjects, which I have already laid out for you, and we will... How do I put this? How about, for the duration of our mission together, nobody is sleeping with anybody, nobody has to be nice to anybody, and nobody has to believe anybody else's version of ancient history?"

"Meaning," Ryan said darkly, "that we are not going to discuss any of the things that are really important?"

Lockett paused. "Since you put it that way... Exactly."

"I don't think—"

"Please, Ryan, do things my way just once, for a change of pace, okay?" She started up the stairs to the bedroom. "Besides, I'm too tired to bicker about this right now. I need a nap." But she turned back with a more conciliatory look on her face. "It will be better this way, and we may even be able to be in the same place for more than five minutes without killing each other. If you want to work with me, those are my rules."

Nobody is sleeping with anybody, nobody has to be nice to anybody, and nobody has to believe anybody else's version of ancient history....

He supposed he could live with that. Because he now had another reason to stick it out and keep this partnership going. Somehow, he was going to convince

Lockett that he had never tried to sell her out. Somehow, he had to make her believe that he had not been the one who had given up on their marriage.

Whether it was pride, or integrity, or just plain ego, he was determined to make her see the truth. Somehow.

Chapter Nine

Scandal Sheets

What a night. Lockett rolled over onto her other side,
trying to do it quietly so that it didn't disturb Ryan.

Hours ago, she had abandoned the hideous clothes
he'd bought, content with just the T-shirt and the scrap
of lace underwear that had started out as sinful wedding night lingerie.

She had a choice of either wearing this strange outfit
or putting back on the bustier with attached tulle and
taffeta petticoats specially made to fit under her wedding gown. Unfortunately, the bustier part was tight
and uncomfortable, and the petticoats were stiff and
scratchy.

Not for the first time, she wished she'd been common enough to have worn a regular old bra and panties, maybe even a slip, with her wedding attire. But no,
she had to have designer originals, good for absolutely
nothing in the real world.

So now she was stuck with nothing to wear, crammed
into a teeny-tiny stagecoach next to her ex-husband. He
had worn his jeans to bed, as if he didn't trust her not

to attack him when he fell asleep if he wore anything less. Fat chance.

But he'd taken off his shirt, and the sheet had twisted around him at about the waist. Even in this dim, murky darkness, she could see his bare torso gleaming smooth and muscular over there.

She sighed.

Aside from the obvious space problems, it was hot inside this ridiculous thing. He seemed to be sleeping. She wished she could.

Lockett sighed again, punched her pillow, and then turned back over the first way.

"Lockett . . ." Ryan braced himself up on one elbow. "Every time you move, this whole thing jiggles."

"Well, I'm sorry. But it's hardly my fault."

"Just pick one position and stick to it, okay?"

"I can't sleep," she told him, hiking herself up until she was half sitting, propped against the back wall of the rickety coach. She arranged the sheet tightly around her waist, and then kicked one foot out the side of the covers to cool herself off. "It's really stuffy in here. Whoever came up with this thing was just plain dumb to think anyone could sleep like this. I certainly don't think real cowboys slept in stagecoaches."

"Maybe you'd have liked a couple of bedrolls and a campfire better?" Ryan asked dryly. "With a coyote sniffing around just to make it realistic?"

"Sounds like fun."

"Besides, I don't think they planned on people sleeping in here."

"Well, what were they supp . . ." Her voice died out. "Oh, I get it. But surely even guests of the Honeymoon Haven have to sleep sometime."

"Not if they're smart," he muttered. "Will you please at least try, Lockett? Quit wiggling around, okay?"

"Okay, okay."

"Good." He closed his eyes and turned away, offering a full view of his strong, hard, tanned back.

She remembered waking up next to Ryan, back when they were young and foolish. She remembered counting the indentations on his spine, top to bottom, pressing her lips to each dip as she went down, seeing how many kisses she could drop before he woke up and stopped her with kisses of his own.

"Those were the days," she murmured, gazing hungrily at his back.

"Quiet over there," he commanded.

"Sorry."

She wondered if Ryan would like it if she tangled a leg over there and made a few advances. Would he jump at the chance, like he had last night at his place? Or would he be more sensible now, like she was trying to be, and realize that sex alone wasn't going to solve anything, no matter how much fun they had trying?

Just because the old sparks were still there didn't mean it was anything but insane to act on it. She and Ryan had already proved to both their satisfaction that they were no good for each other. When she thought of how many obstacles stood in the way of any possible liaison, it made her want to jump off the nearest cliff.

First, there was the small matter of their shared past, when he had proven he couldn't be trusted, and so had she. He had betrayed her trust by offering to annul her for the money, and she had betrayed his trust by running out on him without giving him a chance to defend himself. Not that there was the slightest thing he could have said in defense, but still . . . Maybe she should've tried.

And now there was the problem of her father and fiancé on the warpath looking for her, and Ryan's mysterious connections to his uncle Max, who she felt was the moral equivalent of Genghis Khan.

What future could there possibly be for two people as mixed-up and confused as the two of them? When her marriage to Ryan broke up, she swore she would never let her emotions overrule her good sense again. She had broken that rule exactly once. Last night when she went looking for him after the bachelorette party. And look how far that had gotten her.

No, she wasn't going to break it again. She was going to be reasonable and sensible and keep her hands to herself. And she was also going to get some sleep.

She slid back down into the bed, trying to find some position that was comfortable. But every time she moved an inch to the left, she slammed into the outer shell of the coach. And every time she edged right, she hit some part of Ryan's body.

Restless and moody, she tried to lay as still as possible so as not to rouse him. But she was so hot, and the bed felt lumpy no matter where she moved.

"Ryan," she whispered. "Ryan?"

"What is it now?"

"What would you think of switching sides?" she returned. "You're by the door, and maybe it's cooler on your side."

"I don't care. If it will make you stop all this tossing and turning, it's fine by me."

"Okay. You slide over, and I'll go over the top. Okay?" She rose onto her haunches. "All right. Just scoot over—"

"Oof."

"Hey, wait a min—"

Somehow her elbow ended up in his midriff, he grabbed to catch her before she did any other damage, and she ended up sprawled across his long, lean body. She felt the imprint of his hip against hers, her bare knee riding his waist, his hot hand clutching her bottom.

"Get your hand off my—"

"Move your leg, damn it."

"Don't swear at me."

"Move your leg, Lockett."

She only now realized what exactly her leg was up against. She moved it.

"Sorry," she whispered. "I didn't mean to..."

His eyes were such a dark, dramatic green in the dim light. He was staring at her.

Without thinking it through, she reached out a finger to trace the clean line of his jaw, to brush the softer edge of his bottom lip. He really was a beautiful man.

Inching up to him, she kissed him. He tasted sweet and cool against her mouth. He tasted like banked fires, like passion kept under lock and key. He tasted marvelous.

With her hand still cupping his jaw, she pulled back, just to look at him.

"It's your rule, Lockett," he whispered, but he didn't move. "Nobody sleeps with anybody."

"I know. It's just a hard one to keep."

"You're telling me."

And then he set her away, on the side of the bed she'd traded for, and he hunched back down into the covers.

It was better this way. She would've stopped him, sooner or later. She wouldn't have taken it any further. She just had to see . . .

Cursing, she threw herself down on her new side of the bed, dropping her head into the pillow. It smelled like him, like leather and male skin, like whatever shampoo he used on that long, lovely mane of his.

She jolted over onto her back, where her nose wouldn't be stuck up against the intimacy of his damned scent. Feeling for the open area on the side of the coach, she planned to lie as close as possible to the edge without actually falling out. But her hand hit something on the side of the stagecoach and all of a sudden all hell broke loose.

"What the—"

The coach began to lurch and rock, up and down, back and forth, with a huge, galumphing motion that was quite outrageous.

"Is this an earthquake?" she managed, trying not to bounce around and failing miserably.

"Special effects," Ryan volunteered, catching her neatly as she fell across him again. "It's like magic fingers, only on steroids."

"Magic fingers?"

"Those things they put in cheap motel rooms to make the bed vibrate," he explained. His voice rose and fell with the motion of the carriage. "You stick quarters in to make it go. This one's free at least. It's supposed to be sexy, I guess."

"The things you know about," she said with disgust. "My hand hit something over behind my pillow. Do you think it was the switch?"

"Yeah, I guess. Where?" he asked, trying to maneuver around behind her while the rollicking bed kept throwing them back at each other.

She had been through so much in one twenty-four-hour period, and this was an amazingly stupid way to end up, crashing and bashing in a runaway stagecoach. As Ryan levered across the bed, scrambling to find the switch, Lockett began to laugh. She couldn't help herself. Great, loud peals of laughter bounced off the walls of the carriage as she lay full out, giving her body up to the crazy rhythm.

"It's supposed to be sexy, Lockett," he said as he finally found the switch. "Not funny."

"I can't help it," she cried, doubled-up with giggles. "I keep thinking of two people trying to make love in this contraption. Forget foreplay. Forget subtlety. They'd be exhausted just trying to keep Part A connected to Part B without breaking an arm or a leg."

"You have a very odd sense of humor," he told her, but he pulled her into the crook of his arm and laid back onto the pillows, and for the first time, Lockett began to feel really cozy. "You're safer over here, where I can keep you out of trouble and away from the controls that run the bed."

"Controls? You mean there are more choices than just the runaway stage?" she said with interest.

"Never mind," Ryan said drowsily. His arm tightened around her, and Lockett hoped she had the willpower not to give in to temptation.

WHEN SHE WOKE UP, they were wrapped together like two kittens in a basket.

Just as Ryan began to drift awake, Lockett sat up, scandalized. Quickly she jumped down out of the bed and retreated into the barrel to take a *cold* shower. Maybe she could then start to think more clearly.

After her shower, Lockett eyed Ryan across the remains of a relatively normal breakfast from room service. Well, it would've been normal, except for the fact that they were eating it off the floor. She was going to ask Ryan why there was so little furniture in the suite, until she realized he would just say, "Because people who come to Honeymoon Haven don't need furniture."

Leaning back against the leg of the settee, Lockett gazed at her dark, dangerous ex-husband. She remembered him as a morning person, but today Ryan looked a little bleary. She figured she probably looked worse, but at least it fit their cover story. Real newlyweds couldn't possibly look this worn out and used up.

"Well, partner, what's first on the agenda?" she asked as brightly as she could manage.

He pushed away his plate, rising to his feet. "A plan might be nice."

She shrugged. "True enough. Have you got one?"

"We need to lay our cards on the table."

"We don't have a table," she said with a spark of mischief.

Ryan ignored her little joke. Intently he asked, "Listen, Lockett, why do you think your father insisted you marry Marsh?"

"I really don't know."

"Okay, well, let's think of some possible reasons."

She waited. "Okay." He didn't offer any. "I don't know, Ryan. I was hoping you'd have a few theories."

"I do."

"Well?" she prompted. "I thought we were laying our cards on the table."

"First on the list..." Ryan ran a hasty hand through his hair, as if he really didn't want to tell her what he thought.

"Spit it out," she ordered.

"Money."

"Money?"

"Money."

"But my father has so much, he doesn't know what to do with it," she told him. "And besides, a wedding *costs* a small fortune. What's the gain there?"

"Well, it could be that Stanford was going to pay your father for the privilege of getting you," Ryan said with a certain edge. "Maybe your fiancé was the highest bidder for your hand."

"I don't think so." Lockett pulled down her T-shirt, her total wardrobe at this point, and pushed herself up onto the settee. Once situated, she tilted back, gazing at the ceiling. "For one thing, Stanford doesn't have that much money. He's got a great future, don't get me wrong, but not a lot of liquid assets. And besides, Daddy would not need his money."

"I have reason to believe that your father suffered some serious financial problems about six months ago," Ryan said carefully. "Does knowing that change your mind?"

"Do you know that for sure?" She nervously scrambled to a sitting position. "Is it really true that my father had financial reverses?"

"I think so. If my information is accurate."

"Information from Uncle Max?"

Ryan narrowed his eyes. "Is that a problem?"

"Only if we think we can't trust his information. Come on, Ryan. Stop being so touchy." She absolutely refused to argue with him. It got them nowhere. "So it was your uncle who told you?"

"Let's just say I'm not choosy about my sources if it gets me the information I need."

"So it *was* Uncle Max?"

Ryan offered no response.

"Okay. Given your charming attitude, I am going to assume that Uncle Max told you that my dad had some deals that went south." Ignoring Ryan's stormy expression, she chewed her lip, her mind racing to put the pieces together. "These are big deals, right?"

"Big enough."

"Okay." With this as a purely academic puzzle, Lockett was enjoying it a bit more. When she thought of it connected to her family, actually pushing people to commit desperate acts, it made her feel queasy. But if she pretended it was an Agatha Christie novel, she could handle it. "His entire company is based on trust—I mean, that's what he does, manages money for his clients. So I suppose if he lost a large amount of money, especially other people's investments, it could put him in a vulnerable position."

"And what would he do to get out of that situation?" Ryan asked.

She shrugged. "Get more capital and invest it again. Hope that he makes a killing in order to pay off the money he lost in the first place."

"And where would he get a large amount of money?"

"Well," she said emphatically, "not from Stanford. He works for my father. I told you, he wouldn't have that kind of cash."

"What if he married you?" Ryan asked suddenly, and Lockett could tell he thought he was on to something. "Would he be entitled to your money?"

"So you think my father and Stanford concocted this deal where my fiancé would loan Dad money from my accounts?" She shook her head doubtfully. "My inheritance is locked up tight in trust funds. I'm sure it's all husband-proof. *I* can't even touch it. Although there is one other trust fund that does change when I marry..."

"Yeah?"

"It's from my grandmother whom I'm named after. I'm supposed to come into it when I get married, but still, it doesn't really fit into your theory," she explained. "Dad's company already manages the trust, and he has to know I wouldn't move it. I'm not sure I can touch it, even if I want to. I think the only difference is that I get income from it after I'm married. Whereas right now, I can't touch any of it. Even the income just feeds back into the trust."

"This sounds very promising."

"I really don't think so."

But Ryan was on a roll. He strode back and forth in front of her. "How much money are we talking about?"

"In the original trust, you mean?"

He nodded.

"Several million, I would guess. But I really don't know what income to expect. That would only start..."

"After you got married." Turning back for a moment, Ryan raised a dark brow. "But you've already been married. How come you didn't come into this trust fund when you married me?"

"I never asked for it," she said vaguely. Back in those tumultuous days, the last thing on her mind was some dusty trust fund set up by a long-dead grandmother. "Besides, our marriage was annulled pretty fast. Back to square one."

His gaze was intent. "All these years, I thought you got a quickie divorce."

"Does it really matter? So I got a quickie annulment instead," she returned with an evasive shrug. "Daddy didn't want anyone to know the marriage had ever happened. An annulment seemed like the best way to go at the time."

"Glad to hear it was all so easy for you." His voice was light, but she detected a hint of bitterness lurking just under the surface.

"Tony, we said we weren't going to talk about this, remember? Water under the bridge."

It wasn't until after she'd said it that she realized what she'd called him. She didn't understand why all of a sudden her brain had unexpectedly fed her the name of the boy she had once loved. Tony...the perfect lover.

Lockett took a deep breath, wondering if he had noticed.

"Look," he said suddenly with an air of distraction. "I'm going out. I'll find you some better clothes and pick up some other things. While I'm gone, why don't you figure out how we can get some details on that trust fund of yours?"

"That's easy. All I have to do is call—"

"No phone calls," he interrupted. "They can trace us."

"I wouldn't call anyone who couldn't be trusted," she protested.

"No phone calls," Ryan said again with more authority this time.

And then he was gone.

Lockett waited a good five minutes before she picked up the phone. She didn't care what Ryan said. For one thing, he had no right to order her around. And for another, she knew who she could trust.

He picked up on the first ring. That was Charlie, always at his desk.

"Don't say anything," she began. "It's Lockett."

There was silence.

"Are you there?"

"Yes, I'm here," he whispered. "You told me not to say anything."

"Well, you can say hello."

"Hello. How are you? What in the hell is going on?" She could just see Charlie spinning around in his chair, the receiver pressed to his ear. It was great to hear a familiar voice. "This place is going crazy with stories about the wedding of the century blown to smithereens, rod-up-the-spine Stanford Marsh left at the aisle, Old Man Kensington having hissy fits, and no Lockett anywhere. You sure do know how to stir up drama, don't you?"

"I try, I try." She smiled. "Let me just tell you that I am fine, that I am better than fine, because I didn't want to get married anyway."

"Amen to that. So," he said, sounding very conspiratorial, "where are you? What's the real scoop? I heard you ran away with a male stripper, but Accounting has even money on a kidnapping/brainwash. Personnel is leaning toward a sex change in Switzerland, but I told them they were crazy."

"Bet against strippers, kidnappings and sex changes. I'll tell you everything when I come home." She wished she had a watch. She wanted to make sure she didn't talk long enough to be traced. But how long was that? "Right now, I haven't got much time, and I need your help."

"Anything I can do. I'm all yours."

"I wish." Charlie was a dear, dear friend, but they'd known years ago there would never be a romance between them. "Charlie, do you work on my trust fund at all?"

"Sorry," he said with a sigh. "Old Man Kensington handles the family accounts personally. Peons like me don't even see them. Although I think your former fiancé Stanford might have been elevated to status sufficient to get his paws on them when he got his last promotion."

"When was that?"

"I don't know. About a year ago. Maybe a little more."

About a year ago was when they'd started dating. Was it a coincidence? Or was there really something to this trust fund idea? "Listen, Charlie, how do I find out more about it? If I want to see the paperwork on my trust, how would I do that?"

"Well, call your father, I guess."

"That's sort of out of the question at the moment," she said dryly.

"How about his secretary? Her files are something to behold," Charlie said helpfully. "Either on her computer, or in her cabinets. If this company handles it, it should all be there."

"Great. Can you get in there?"

"Me?" He laughed shortly. "That lady's a dragon. She'd scratch out the eyes of anybody who even breathed on her files. I can get as far as her desk, but she'll kick me out before I'm near anything useful."

"I can't think of any way—"

"Thanks for calling." Charlie's voice became much brisker and more businesslike all of a sudden. "I'll take care of that for you right away, Mr. Ellsworth. Call anytime, you hear? Anytime."

And he hung up on her. Clearly, someone important, like maybe her father or her ex-fiancé, had been lurking nearby.

Lockett chewed on her fingernail, trying to mull this over. She would have to see the paperwork on her trust fund. But how? Nobody was going to hand it to her. So that meant she had to get into the Kensington Building.

And for that, she needed her sister. Beatie had a private line in her room, and Lockett knew she wasn't likely to be up yet. The phone rang a few times, but finally a sleepy voice answered.

"Beatie, rise and shine. It's your big sis."

"Lockett?" Beatie gasped. "Where are you? Are you okay?"

"I'm fine. I haven't got much time. Listen, okay?" She spoke softly but urgently into the phone. "Get some of my clothes and some of yours. An assortment of my things, but I only need one outfit of yours. Something that will fit me well, and something that looks young."

"Young?"

"You know, trendy."

"Okay," Beatie said doubtfully.

"Stick the clothes in a plastic garbage bag, and leave the bag in the Dumpster behind Dad's building in the Loop. Have you got that?"

"Wait, wait, I'm writing it down. Your clothes, mine, garbage bag, Dumpster... Okay. What else?" her sister asked frantically.

"Just one more thing—your driver's license. If anybody asks, you can say it was lost or stolen or something. That ought to do it."

"Okay. I guess. Am I supposed to do this right now?"

"Not this instant." Lockett figured she'd better make her break-in to the Kensington Building after dark, which left hours for Beatie's mission. If she did it too early, someone was likely to steal Lockett's precious garbage bag. "Around seven. Can you do that?"

"Sure. Do you need anything else?"

"Well, yeah." She leaned back into the settee. "Money would be great. My hairbrush, too. And shampoo and conditioner. Underwear. Oh, and shoes. Lots of shoes—"

Across the Ride 'Em Cowboy Suite, the door began to open. Lockett sat up hastily, dropping the receiver into the cradle and kicking the entire phone under the chair. And then she acted nonchalant.

"Hi," she said brightly as Ryan walked in. "How did it go?"

"Not so great." His arms were full of packages, but he tossed a newspaper down in front of her first.

With the front page staring her in the face, Lockett saw... her face.

Kensington Heiress Kidnapped, the headline blared. Her eyes wide, Lockett snatched it up and scanned the story.

"'Only hours before her wedding,'" she read out loud, "'Lockett Kensington was escorted from her parents' luxurious Lake Forest home, apparently at gunpoint.'" She glanced up. "At gunpoint, did you hear that? Puh-leez. And this is a terrible picture of me. It's my publicity shot from cochairing the Orchestra Ball. I never did like that picture."

"You should be glad it's not a better likeness," Ryan offered.

Ignoring him, she kept reading the story. "'Catering assistants reportedly saw a suspicious figure peering into windows sometime before the alleged kidnapping...'" She cringed. "That must've been me when I was sneaking back into the house. I didn't think anyone saw me."

"It gets better. Read on."

She skimmed a few paragraphs. "'At a press conference this morning, Elliot Farnham Kensington III, father of the missing woman, is expected to announce that the FBI has been called in...'" She glanced up at Ryan's grim face. "The FBI? How can they do this?"

"Easy. If Elliot Kensington says there's been a kidnapping, there's been one."

"But he has to expect me to surface and tell everyone it's a lie." She searched Ryan's face. "There's no way this can work."

"I don't know, Lockett. But with the FBI looking for us..."

"I'll tell them I'm not kidnapped." She reached for the telephone. "I'll call the newspapers and the police and tell them this is a big hoax."

"I don't think that's a good idea at all—"

But before she had even picked up the receiver, the phone began to ring.

The sound grew more insistent.

Lockett stared down at the phone in her hand, Ryan stared at her, and the telephone just kept ringing away, cheery as you please.

Lockett took a deep breath.

Chapter Ten

Close Quarters

"Hello?"

"Lockett? You sound weird. Why did you hang up on me?"

"Beatie." She sank back into the settee with relief. To Ryan, she said, "It's okay—it's just my sister." Into the phone, she added, "Sorry. Something came up."

"Your sister?" Ryan growled. "How the hell does your sister know where to call you? I'm not gone five minutes and you're already telegraphing your whereabouts to the folks at home? Why didn't you just call your father directly and save everybody some time?"

"I didn't tell her where I was," she whispered to him with her hand over the mouthpiece. Back into the phone, she asked, "Beatie, how did you call me back? I didn't give you a number. I didn't tell you where to call."

"Oh," Beatie said calmly, "I just used that automatic call-back button. It just rings back whoever called you last."

"Great," she muttered.

"Anyway, I thought you should know." Beatie dropped her voice. "Lockett, they're telling people that you were kidnapped, and that your crazy ex-husband did it. They're making Ryan sound like a stalker or something."

The news continued to get worse.

"Lockett, what should I do?" Beatie asked. "Should I go talk to the police myself? I can tell them Ryan is no stalker."

"No. Stay out of it," she said quickly. "I need you. If Dad knows you're on my side, he'll probably send you to boarding school in Switzerland. Just stay calm. We need you where you are."

"Okay." Beatie's voice was doubtful. "Do you still want the garbage bag and all the other stuff?"

"Yes, I do." She glanced up at Ryan, who was still obviously angry, and was still in the dark about the plotting she'd done while he was out. "At seven. Behind Dad's building in the Loop."

"Okay. And, Lockett?"

"Yes?"

Beatie hesitated. "Be careful, will you? I don't want you or Ryan getting shot at or anything, just because Mother and Dad have lost their marbles."

"Okay. Thanks, Beatie." Talking to her sister made her very homesick for the days when driving Beatie to her tennis lesson was the most stressful thing in Lockett's day. With a sigh, she added, "You'd better call someone else as soon as you hang up. Erase my number off your automatic call-back button, okay?"

And with that, Beatie was gone.

"Are you going to tell me what the hell is going on? Or are you going to chitchat with your sister all day?" Ryan asked fiercely.

Lockett regarded him coolly. "I was not chitchatting. I was putting a plan in motion."

"Damn it, Lockett, I told you not to use the phone while I was gone."

"It was important," she told him, dodging the central issue. "And I found out some crucial information."

"And look what happened. Your little sister, who is living in the same house as your father, who wants to cut me up in little pieces and hog-tie you to Stanford Marsh, now knows where we are." Ryan stopped ranting long enough to rub his forehead wearily. "Get your stuff. We have to be out of here before the cops arrive."

Lockett stayed where she was. "Beatie doesn't know where we are," she insisted. "She just did one of those automatic redial things on her phone. She's certainly not going to tell my father that she talked to me, and I really don't think he'll trace her line. He wouldn't think I'd be stupid enough to call my own house when I'm on the lam."

"I can't believe you're that dumb, either," Ryan muttered.

"I had to talk to her." Lockett grabbed for the bag he'd brought in, quickly riffling through the contents. "Jeans," she said happily. "And tennis shoes. This is great. I was afraid I was going to have to leave wearing nothing but your T-shirt."

"Any place special you were planning on going?"

"That's what I was going to tell you, if you'd stop yelling at me long enough to listen." She hopped into the jeans as she dressed him down. It was not the most formidable position from which to argue, but she was so tired of running around half-naked she didn't care.

The jeans gapped around her waist, obviously way too big. How big did he think she was? She eyed him suspiciously.

"What?" he began. "What's wrong now?"

"Why did you buy me these huge jeans?"

He just stared at her, openmouthed. "I have no idea, okay? I just held 'em up and they looked right. With everything else we have to worry about, you're mad because I picked the wrong size?"

"I just can't imagine anyone thinking that I would wear this big a size, that's all." After glaring at him for a moment, she said, "All right. Let's just forget about it, shall we? But you might want to look a little more closely next time. I've never worn anything above a size six in my life, just for your information."

"Are you ever going to get around to telling me why you had to talk to your sister and what you found out that was so important?" he demanded.

"Well, first I talked to a friend of mine at my father's company, and he—"

"You did what? Not one incredibly foolish phone call, but *two?*"

"It was important. And I told you, if you remember, that I was only going to call people I could trust." She pulled an Indiana Pacers T-shirt and baseball cap out of another bag. "Great disguise. No one would recognize me in this stuff."

"Get on with it," he said, practically steaming. "I'm waiting for an explanation."

"Right." She refused to be cowed. She knew what she'd done was perfectly reasonable, no matter how many nasty glances Ryan sent her way. "I called Charlie, who is a very old and dear friend, and I asked him how a person would go about getting a look at the papers relating to my trust fund. The one you were so interested in?''

"Yes," he returned.

"Right. So Charlie told me those papers are kept in my father's office, under the eagle eye of his dragon lady secretary." Confidentially she added, "I know the woman. A house fell on her sister in *The Wizard of Oz.*"

"What?"

It was a little joke, which obviously he didn't get. "Never mind. Anyway, she's a real witch. There's no way Charlie can get a look at anything while she's there, and besides, I don't want him to get into trouble by trying anything suspicious. So I think the key is for us— you and me—to sneak in after hours and pry open the files. We can look at whatever we want," she finished up smartly.

"Lockett . . ."

"Yes?"

"Nothing. It's not that bad an idea," he admitted. "So I suppose you also have a plan that gets us into the building?"

"As a matter of fact, I do." She slapped the Pacers baseball hat down on top of her head. "That's where Beatie comes in. She's leaving me a disguise, in a garbage bag in the Dumpster behind my father's building."

"What kind of a disguise?" he asked slowly.

"Her clothes." Lockett's lips curved into a mischievous smile. "I'm going to walk right in the front door and sign the after-hours register. I'm going to be Beatie. Pretty nifty idea, huh?"

"THIS IS NEVER going to work," Ryan said darkly.

He pulled his bike over into a parking space on

Adams Street, just a few blocks from the Kensington Building on West Jackson. Lockett quickly hopped off.

"Oh, be quiet. It's a great plan. As Beatie, no one will think it's odd at all for me to be visiting the office. We'll be in and out without a hitch." She sent him a superior glance. "You just don't like being my chauffeur."

"You always get to be the boss, and I end up the servant," he muttered, but she thought she caught a glint of humor in his eyes before he hid them behind dark sunglasses.

She thought he looked pretty cute in the snappy uniform and driver's cap, although she wasn't sure about the ponytail. But he wasn't going to cut off all his hair for a few hours' masquerade as a working stiff, so she supposed the ponytail would have to do.

She, too, was wearing sunglasses, which seemed pretty silly in the lengthening shadows between skyscrapers. But with her picture in all the papers, she needed to be careful.

Lockett raced ahead, trying to pretend she wasn't with him in case they passed any pedestrians. A chauffeur tagging along with an exceedingly casual girl in a baseball cap and baggy jeans would've looked very suspicious. But, as it happened, she didn't pass any pedestrians. The streets of the financial district were empty as she headed toward the all-important Dumpster.

With Ryan lagging behind as lookout, Lockett passed right by the polished red-granite skyscraper where her father plotted his complicated financial dealings. She didn't even give it a glance, just ambled on, until she hit the alley between it and the next building.

As if she hadn't a care in the world, she cut in. It was a skinny little thing, built to barely allow room for deliveries, as well as to give access to the executive parking ramp in the back. The ramp just happened to be right next to a garbage Dumpster, and Lockett headed there like a shot.

Ryan was still back at the entrance to the alley as she pried open the lid of the nasty thing. She could get it open, but keeping it that way long enough to reach in was trickier.

"Pssst," she hissed, averting her nose from the Dumpster. "Hey, you, Mr. Chauffeur. I need you to hold this thing open."

He didn't look happy about it, but he came, anyway, sunglasses in hand, giving her the full benefit of his sulky gaze. With one eye on her, he propped open the lid. "How sure are you that nobody is going to be working late?"

"Very. They all bolt at five-thirty on the button. Even the stragglers will be long gone by now."

Shuddering at the smell emanating from the steamy garbage tank, Lockett quickly boosted herself up far enough to survey the contents. "Trust Beatie to bring a bag with my name on it," she said under her breath.

She pulled at the top of the black plastic bag, where a note card that read, "For Lockett" had been tied. Heaving, she got the thing up and over the edge, down onto the concrete.

"I thought she was leaving you a disguise," Ryan mumbled. He cast a baleful eye at the stuffed bag. "What's all that stuff?

"Just some things I needed." Lockett ripped off the note card and tore into the bag. She pushed past the cosmetics, neatly arranged in little plastic bags, down to the clothes. Beatie's outfit stood out immediately.

It was perfect for a fashion-conscious babe from Generation X. There was an incandescent yellow-and-white striped crop top, a flippy, extremely short black skirt with suspenders and fringe around the hem, and a pair of anklets with black bows on the cuffs.

Rooting all the way down to the bottom, Lockett found shoes, too. Clunky, black lace-up boots with thick soles, just right for a day on a construction site.

"Turn around," she ordered as she started to pull the skirt on over her jeans.

"You're going to change your clothes in an alley?"

"Where else am I supposed to do it? Besides, no one is going to see me." She pushed him with one hand, forcing him to turn away. "Not even you. You just keep an eye out, and if anybody comes, I'll run around behind the Dumpster."

Hopping on one foot, she held the skirt up and kicked out of the jeans. This wasn't going to be pleasant, she realized as she fastened the waist. She and Beatie might wear the same size, but in this skirt, she could feel a definite breeze teasing her bottom.

Oh, well. There was no way around it. She'd asked for young and trendy, hadn't she?

It was more of a struggle to get the crop top on under her T-shirt, but she managed with a bit of huffing and puffing. Then she wobbled into socks and shoes one foot at a time.

Brushing her hair into her face with her fingers, she announced, "Ready."

Ryan spun around slowly, scanning her up and down. "I don't think Beatie fills out that outfit in quite the same way," he said in a choked sort of voice.

His gaze seemed to have stuck at the point where the stretchy little top clung to the curves of her breasts. Lockett flushed. She hadn't realized it was quite so tight. She tugged at it, but that only made the situation worse, only made the spark in Ryan's eyes flame higher.

"No one will be looking at your face, that's for sure," he murmured.

"Well, uh," she mumbled, licking her lip, crossing her arms in a vain attempt to cover up more of her chest, "time to get this show on the road."

"Right."

Grim and stoic, Ryan stuck his sunglasses back on, stowed the garbage bag safely behind the Dumpster, and motioned for her to lead.

This time they were going in the front of the Kensington Building, as bold as brass. Sticking her nose in the air, Lockett waltzed in the doors, right up to the guard's desk, where she trailed one arm over the after-hours register.

"Hi," she said breezily, in a chirpy little voice that sounded nothing like Beatie's. The important thing was that it didn't sound like Lockett, either. She leaned over the desk, giving him a close-up view of her cleavage, which was actually rather impressive in this skimpy top. It was disgusting, but it had to be done. "I'm Beatrice Kensington. I'm supposed to meet my dad up on the executive level. Do I just sign in here?"

"I don't have any note about that, Miss, uh, Kensington, ma'am," the guard stuttered. His young face was quite pink, especially the tips of his ears, and he seemed to be staring a hole in the counter, safely below any point on Lockett's body.

"Oh, well, that's okay," she responded carelessly. She scrawled "B. Kensington" in big round letters across the next empty line on the list. "I know how to get up there. C'mon, James," she said, signaling to Ryan. She leaned in to whisper to the poor, dumbstruck guard, "My driver's coming with me. Thanks!"

And then she danced over to the elevators, giving the guard plenty of opportunity to ogle the fringe barely covering her backside. She could sense Ryan steaming behind her, but she ignored him until they were safely in the elevator.

"A real chauffeur would not be staring daggers at his employer," she told him.

"A real employer would not be twitching her pretty little bottom under the nose of an adolescent security guard," he returned.

"It got us in here, didn't it?"

"That was crude, Lockett. Really bad."

"Oh, please," she scoffed. "What are you, my keeper? You're not my husband anymore, Ryan. Did you forget that?"

"No," he said abruptly. "That's something I never forget."

She crossed her arms over her chest, tapping her foot until the elevator doors finally, ponderously, slid open on the top floor of the Kensington Building.

"This way," she ordered, veering right and stalking past a posh receptionist's desk.

"You probably want to keep it quiet," Ryan said softly, "just in case any of the cleaning staff is hanging around."

"Who cares?" Lockett's nose rose even higher. "I'm Beatrice Kensington. I have a perfect right to be here."

In a light, cynical tone, Ryan offered, "That's fine. Just as long as nobody checks on your story or calls dear old dad to confirm it."

But she had already reached the heavy mahogany door bearing a brass plaque with her father's name on it. Resolute, she pushed it open, revealing a still, eerie, dark office full of all kinds of disturbing shadows. Her heart had been beating more quickly than usual ever since she'd started this caper, but the sight of her father's empty office, his citadel, pushed her pulse into overdrive.

She forced herself to breathe evenly, to hold back the palpitations. It was just an office, after all, just the outer area where the dragon lady sat. Neither her father nor the unreasonable tyrant he'd turned into, would be dropping by. She hoped.

"Dear old dad is too busy telling lies to the FBI to take phone calls or pop into his office just now," she said out loud.

"Let's hope so."

Quickly, quietly, they got to work. It didn't take them long to discover that the filing cabinets in the outer office were all locked, and that a penknife, which Ryan conveniently happened to carry, would pry them open.

Lockett began to scan documents, while Ryan tried to crack the computer. Unfortunately, the Kensington family had many investments, and even though she found file folders with her name on them, she hadn't gotten to her maternal grandmother's trust fund yet.

Ryan had no better luck at the computer. Laying his chauffeur hat aside, he wiped his brow and started to swear at the computer. Lockett wasn't surprised; who in the world could second-guess Elliot Kensington's secretary?

"I can't get in," Ryan said bleakly. "Now I can't even get it to give me the password page. It says I've tried too many times, to go away and not come back."

"Nothing here, either." Lockett slid the last file back into the cabinet. "Every other trust fund in the family is here, but not the one from my grandmother."

"Which is a clue all by itself. If there really is something funny about that file, it makes sense your father would put it someplace safer," Ryan suggested.

Lockett raised an eyebrow. "I really don't think you can make that kind of assumption based on the simple fact that it's not here. He also could've taken it out to check it or update it, because I was getting married."

"Still looking on the bright side, are we?"

"Still looking," she said sweetly. "Is your penknife handy? I think we should go for the inner office next."

Ryan slipped out of his chair and over to the door to Elliot Kensington's personal office. "This one doesn't need the penknife. A credit card will do."

As easily as that, he whipped out a card and jiggled the door open.

"You and your magic credit cards," she noted. "Remind me to get a look at those things sometime. No names on them, untraceable, and they open doors, too."

"I thought my finances were off-limits during the truce," he reminded her.

"Your finances *and* Uncle Max, both taboo. And I have a feeling they're both involved in the mystery of your credit cards." Lockett wished she knew exactly how it all added up. Damn it—it was her idea to ban those subjects from discussion. What had she been thinking of?

But there was no time for that now. The mystery of her trust fund needed to be solved first.

Lockett doused the lights in the outer office; just in case anyone happened by, they didn't want light showing under the door. Relocking the outside doors, carefully closing the inner door behind her, she stole into the inner sanctum, where Ryan was already starting to search.

"Desk drawer was open—nothing in there," he reported. Standing in front of a massive leather chair, he swept his arm to indicate the vast expanse of her father's desk. "No filing cabinets, no folders, a clean desk."

She remembered this office from occasional visits when she was younger, although she hadn't been there in a while. "There was never anything in here but the desk and the chair, as I recall. We thought it was weird, when I was a kid. Just a desk stuck in the middle of this huge, empty office. Except for the paintings on the walls. But even they look kind of lonely with all this empty space."

Dismissing the huge canvases of modern art on three sides, Ryan pulled the drapes. All that revealed was a large window and a sparkling skyline, spanning almost the whole outside wall.

"Nothing back here, either. Where would he put important papers? They have to be somewhere." As he circled the room, he began to tap the walls with his knuckles.

"Are you looking for a safe?" she inquired.

Ryan shrugged. "Maybe."

"Well, I know where that is."

"Why didn't you say so?"

"You didn't ask." Lockett crossed to the most outlandish painting, a big splotch of magenta against a yellow background. So far it had been like a game. But for some reason, offering up her father's safe made it feel more like a betrayal. She had to put herself on automatic pilot and just open the damn thing.

"He showed me this when I was a kid." She flipped the painting back from the wall with a telltale creak of hinges, displaying a small, square safe. As if it were no big thing, she explained, "He showed it to me because the combination was my birthday. You know, go to Daddy's office, sit in the big chair, see how the safe works. Cute, huh? He might have changed it by now, but I doubt it. The combination had been my birth date as long as the safe was here."

"If he was that open about his safe," Ryan said slowly, "do you really think he would leave anything important in there?"

She shrugged. Why was he asking all these questions? Couldn't he see how difficult this was for her?

Retreating once more into cynicism, she asked flippantly, "Who knows? The man I grew up with didn't have anything to hide. But the one who told me I had to get married or he'd lock me in my room for the rest of my life might very well be hiding something."

Ryan's eyes held her, and she thought she might've even caught a note of compassion there. As quickly as she saw it, it had faded. No, she didn't really think she would see sympathy for anything relating to her father in Ryan's eyes. Too much bad blood there.

"You'd better open it," he said.

Willing her fingers to work quickly, Lockett spun the dial—6-1-69. Her birth date. As smooth as silk, the tumblers clicked into place and the door swung open.

She stepped back. "Be my guest."

Ryan didn't need to be asked twice. He stuck his hands in there and pulled out a pile of papers that he passed to Lockett.

"Old letters," she said, paging through the stack. "The deed for the house in Lake Forest. My birth certificate. Beatie's. Marriage license. This isn't what we're looking for, Ryan."

"Bingo."

"What? What did you find?"

His voice was low and urgent, threaded with excitement. "A file folder marked 'Elizabeth Templeton, nee Lockett, grantor, in trust for Lockett Elizabeth Kensington . . .'"

"That's it." She reached for it, trying to flip it open and read the contents, while Ryan hastily searched through the rest of the safe's contents.

"Stock certificates and some cash, too. But here are a few things that look more interesting," he murmured, removing them one at a time and tucking them into his waistband for safekeeping.

"Hmm?" She looked up. "What did you say?"

But Ryan went very still. "Did you hear anything?" he whispered. "Was that a door?"

Click. Definitely a door. And now there were voices, too.

Male voices.

Someone was in the outer office.

Chapter Eleven

Roman Rhapsody

Lockett looked to Ryan. Swiftly, noiselessly, he swung the safe and the painting back into place. He hit the light switch, and then hesitated a moment very near the door, as if he were listening.

Lockett stood frozen. What should she do? Where could they go?

The plot to break into her father's office had started out as fun and games, but suddenly things seemed a bit more ominous. Not only might there really be something shady about her trust fund, but now she and Ryan were caught, like rats in a trap, while whoever was in the outer office just marched in and collared them.

The voices grew louder, closer. Ryan gestured in the direction of the desk, but she didn't understand.

And then he grabbed her, hustling her and the precious folder over, shoving them into the niche under her father's desk. He rolled in after her.

Just as they heard the door scrape open, just as the voices crossed over the threshold, Ryan stretched out a foot, slowly, soundlessly, easing the big leather chair in closer, until it was blocking them in, covering their hiding place.

The lights switched on.

"Why are the drapes open?" her father's voice asked. Heavy footsteps paced right past them, inches from the desk, and she heard the clatter and swoosh of the drapes being pulled.

Lockett huddled next to Ryan, too afraid to breathe. She was clutching the file so tightly her fingers started to cramp, but she didn't dare move them for fear of rustling the papers or bumping the desk.

"What have you heard?" another voice asked. It was Stanford. "Anything yet?"

"No," her father said angrily. There was a loud thump as he braced himself on the edge of the desk. "Not a damn thing. But they can't have gone far. We'll find them."

Ryan's face was very close to hers. "It's okay," he mouthed silently. "Sit tight. They'll go away."

She nodded, just barely. She was glad she wasn't under the desk alone, but it was almost worse to be wedged in there with Ryan, like two little oysters in the same clam. Her breast brushed his elbow every time she took the tiniest breath, his long, hard, trouser-clad thigh pressed up against her bare one, and his head bent in so close that she could feel the pressure of his soft, muted breathing ruffling her hair.

Lockett closed her eyes. All she wanted to do was inch over a little closer, into his lap, where he could wrap her in his arms and murmur soothing words.

What was she doing breaking into offices, anyway? She was no criminal.

Well, she was now.

"This is so unlike Lockett," her father grumbled. She couldn't have agreed more. "The only time she ever caused me any problems was when she ran away with that punk the first time. I don't know what he does to her, but the minute he's around her, the trouble starts again."

Next to her in their tiny hiding place, Ryan smiled. He knew he was trouble, and he loved it.

"I told you not to involve him," Stanford snapped. Lockett had never heard him use that tone with her father. This indicated a different balance of power than she would've imagined. "If you hadn't sent people out after him and gotten him all stirred up, we wouldn't be in this mess."

"I did the best I could," her father returned. "I don't care how long they'd been apart, he never would've let Lockett marry you. Never. The only shot I had was to head him off. So it didn't work. It was worth a try."

But Stanford just snorted in contempt. "He stayed away for years. He'd washed his hands of her long ago."

"Stayed away? Ha!" Elliot Kensington shifted his weight, rising from the desk. "He was never very far away. He kept tabs on her, and I kept tabs on him. And we both knew it."

Lockett searched Ryan's face. Was this true? His expression was unreadable.

"Well, now that you've blundered so badly, what are we going to do?" Stanford demanded petulantly.

"Just exactly what we are doing." Her father's footsteps trod across the carpet. If Lockett was any judge, he was nearing the wall with the safe. "We'll find them. We'll throw him in the slammer. And we'll get this wedding back on track."

"How much time do we have?"

"Not enough," her dad said curtly. "Damn Lockett, anyway. We were so close."

There was a soft, small creak, and Lockett knew he had turned the painting aside. The safe. Click. The slide and fall of the tumblers. It would only be another moment before he discovered—

"Good God, Marsh!" her father shouted.

Lockett cringed.

"The trust fund file is missing," he declared, panic evident in his voice. "And the ledgers from Seaboard Development. This is terrible."

"Who could've taken them?"

"Who do you think?" Elliot Kensington exploded. "That damn Ryan. He's got them. It has to be him. Nobody else would dare snatch my papers out from under my nose. He wheedled the combination out of Lockett, and then he came in here and took my files. The arrogance of that punk."

They were in big trouble. She waited for the chair to be torn away, for them to be ripped from their hiding place.

"Will they know what they mean?"

"I don't know. I doubt it. But we can't take the chance."

"What should we do?"

"We have to find them. Now." Her father slammed the safe shut, and his footsteps pounded toward the door. "I want A.P.B.'s everywhere. Not just the kidnapping. We need to up the ante. Let's leak Ryan's past, make it look really bad. Mob connections, trouble with the law—whatever it takes. I'll offer a better reward. Somebody must have seen one or the other of them.

And they can't have gotten far if Ryan was back here today vandalizing my office."

And then the office went black. The door crashed. The voices and the footsteps receded.

Under the desk, Lockett let out the breath she'd been holding since they'd first taken refuge.

"I thought for sure they'd know we were still in the office," she gasped.

Ryan pushed away the heavy chair, angling his long body out from under the desk. "Good thing I'm not claustrophobic," he said as he reached back a hand for Lockett.

"If you were claustrophobic, you wouldn't have lasted five minutes in the Ride 'Em Cowboy bed."

He smiled lazily, pulling her out by the hand, until they were both standing in the dark, shadowy office. "How do you like that, Lockett?" One of his hands cupped her cheek; the other caught her at the waist. "They think I'm behind all of this. Not giving you much credit, are they?"

"There's nothing new about that."

"I'm trying very hard not to underestimate you," he whispered. And then he bent and kissed her, very quickly.

Her own voice came out shaky and a little strained. "Did you really keep tabs on me all these years?"

Regretfully, he pulled away. "Much as I would love to continue this, we haven't got time, sweetheart." He took her by the hand, leading her out of the office. "We have to get out of here before the place is crawling with cops."

"They're gone."

"They'll be back. Fingerprints. Clues." Out in the hall, he looked back and forth. "Is there a stairwell? A back exit, maybe?"

"This way." She headed for the emergency stairs she'd loved to run up and down as a little girl. Quickly she sped down the steps, floor after floor, until she and Ryan were both breathless.

"How much farther?"

"We're here." She pointed to the big red one painted on the door. "First floor."

But before her hand reached the knob, Ryan stopped her. "What does this let out on? Anywhere near the guard's desk?"

"No. We're in the back."

"Do you know how to get out of here without going back past the guard?" he asked quickly.

She nodded. And he wrenched open the door.

The corridor was dark. Her heart pounding, Lockett hoped she remembered where the back door was. But she led him to the end of the hall, and there was no nice, welcome exit there, just the door to the ladies' room and another door marked Cleaning.

Dead end. They were going to have to backtrack.

And then there was a muffled thump from the other direction, from the far end of the hall. A light went on. The end of the hall held a pool of golden light, which was moving about.

It must be the guard with a flashlight.

"Come on," Ryan said softly, pulling her after him into the pitch blackness of the women's rest room.

Once again she was huddled in the darkness, listening to the horrifying sound of approaching footsteps.

"Look," Ryan whispered in her ear. "There's a window."

The two of them crept over together, and Ryan climbed onto the sink to inch the thing open. He poked his head out, and then turned back to her.

"We're right over the Dumpster, about ten feet up. Can you jump?"

She nodded. Her heart was in her throat. She didn't want to jump into the Dumpster, but if the alternative was staying in a dark rest room by herself, she'd jump.

He went first, levering himself out the window. Ryan disappeared.

"Lockett," he called softly from out there somewhere. "Come on. Jump!"

She got up on the sink. She got out far enough to straddle the windowsill. She looked down.

Behind her, she heard a knock on the door.

"Anybody in there?" someone called.

"There comes a time when you have to trust me, Lockett!" Ryan shouted. "I'll catch you. But you have to jump."

She glanced back at the door, and she peered out into the darkness, out to where she thought Ryan would be.

Trust. Never one of her stronger qualities.

She jumped.

"RYAN, I DO NOT WANT to go back there."

"Get on the motorcycle, Lockett." He put his bike in gear and started to ease away from the sidewalk. He was trying hard not to lose his patience, but back at the Dumpster, when she'd refused to leave without her damn garbage bag, he had begun to feel pretty cranky.

He'd saved her back at the window, hadn't he? He'd caught her, as promised. Okay, so it wasn't perfect, but he got them safely out of there. And so what if they had to run through the dark streets of Chicago like bats out of hell? Lockett and her luggage were what slowed them down.

Now, here she stood on the curb, wearing that idiotic outfit her sister put together for her, clutching her big old trash bag, refusing to move.

"Lockett, we know it's safe there. We know they're looking for us here. Every hotel and motel in Chicago is going to get scoured, and probably half of Wisconsin, as well. But that place is farther away. They won't think we're using any place that far away as a base of operations." Tired of trying to convince her, he lost the battle of manners. "Now, damn it, get on the bike, and let's get out of here before the cops arrive."

"But the Ritz is so close." Lockett didn't even know why she was acting like this.

"For you, Ms. Kensington, the Ritz is the first place they'll look."

"I thought your apartment was the first place they'd look."

"Well, after the Ritz."

But she finally consented to climb on behind him. After tying her bag on the back of the bike as well as she could, she wrapped her arms around his waist and settled in.

As aggravated as he was, it felt good to have her back there. He had once thought it would be paradise to tool aimlessly around the country on his bike, with Lockett riding shotgun. They'd stop wherever they felt like, do whatever they wanted, earn enough cash to take them a few more miles, and then off they'd ride, into the sunset, one more time.

Now that they were fugitives, the circumstances were quite not what he had envisioned, but, oddly enough, it still felt right.

The trip was quiet enough back to Indiana. He wondered if maybe she'd fallen asleep back there. But her arms around him were secure and tight, and he had to figure she was just behaving herself for once.

This time, it was quite late when they finally pulled into the parking lot under the blinking neon sign of the almost naked woman.

He didn't know why Lockett disliked the place so much; he kind of got a kick out of it. Was her antipathy just part and parcel of being a spoiled princess? Or maybe its overt sexuality hit her where she lived.

Around Lockett, the issue of sex always had a way of rearing its ugly head.

He knew she wasn't pleased at the sparks still flying between them. He also knew the feelings were intensifying, and every moment they spent in places like the Ride 'Em Cowboy suite, it only got worse.

Mostly, he knew that she was afraid. Hell, so was he. Besides, he had some standards. He didn't want to make love with a woman who couldn't make up her mind. She had been so close to marrying Stanford, when she should've known all along that that would never work. And now here she was with him. Was it because she loved him? Because she'd always loved him?

No. It was because she didn't know who she loved. That was *not* his Lockett. She used to be impulsive and decisive. When it came time to jump, she jumped.

The new Lockett couldn't seem to figure out what she wanted. Although she had shown no signs that she wanted him.

Ryan smiled grimly. Except for in bed, of course.

And he sure as hell didn't want to make love with a woman who didn't trust him. She might jump out of windows for him, but she still believed that, once upon a time, he'd chosen money over the woman he loved.

That wound was still fresh. Ryan turned off the bike. "We're here."

"Please, don't send me back to the Ride 'Em Cowboy suite," she mumbled behind him. But she brought her bag and followed him into that amazing lobby with its doves and cupids and all those fountains.

The same girl, in the same dippy red dress, was standing behind the front desk. "Hi!" she greeted them. "Mr. and Mrs. Haven, right? Gee, are you in the navy? I didn't realize."

"The navy?" The clerk was gazing at his clothes. *Oh, hell.* He had forgotten he was still wearing the chauffeur's outfit, although he'd lost his hat somewhere. *Damn it.* Where was the hat? Blown off halfway back to Illinois, probably.

"Well, Mr. and Mrs. Haven, we're glad to have you again."

"Lucky us," Lockett murmured.

He kicked her. "We enjoyed our first night so much, we decided to come back. Do you have anything available?"

"Hmm. Dungeon o' Desire is still open. Or let's see . . . Oh, this is a good one. I have the Temple of Venus available."

"The Temple of Venus," they both said at once.

This time, as they tripped through Lover's Lagoon, following the trail of orange tiki torches in search of the Ancient Amours building, Lockett seemed somewhat resigned.

He took the big plastic bag away from her, slinging it over his shoulder. The thing was outrageously heavy.

"So this Temple of Venus sounds like something you'd like, huh? Greek, classy?"

"Venus is Roman, not Greek," she informed him. "Aphrodite is the Greek goddess of love. But, hey, I don't expect Honeymoon Haven to know the difference." With a superior smile, she took the key away from him and let herself into the Temple of Venus. "I look at it this way—it can't be any worse than Ride 'Em Cowboy. I mean, what are the chances they'll have saddles and whips?"

She was right, but now there was a lot of white gauzy fabric thrown around and endless pillows. Of course, pillars, also. He stepped through two tall ones, and then took a few steps down into the main area, which was cut out like a bowl in the center of the room.

Not much there, just a bunch of cushy white pillows on the white-and-gold tiled floor, and the requisite hot tub. This one was big and square, with short, fat pedestals at the corners. Something leafy and green was draped around the columns, and creamy white statues of plump young ladies in the buff topped them off. The statues were lit from within, glowing into the dim room, the only source of light.

Lockett was standing by the hot tub, and she turned around a couple of times, scanning the room. "No windows and no walls," she said finally.

And she was right. From the sunken area with the tub, steps led up in each direction. But there were no doors, just sheer white curtains all around.

With a jaded eye, Lockett went to inspect one side, so he took the other.

His side had the bed. Lockett ought to like it—it was plenty big, and very airy. Once he parted the filmy white curtains around it, he saw that the bed itself was pretty much level with the floor. Kneeling down to touch it, he discovered it moved. A giant water bed built into the ground.

Instead of a headboard, there was a huge painting of a nude, fleshy nymph cavorting with a goat in a flowery glade. Well, sort of a goat. He didn't think the painting was Lockett's style at all. He smiled. He couldn't wait for her to get a load of that.

The only other feature of note was what the designer had used to make the posts in the four-poster theme. They were white, just like everything else in the place, but they were also naked ladies, stretching their arms above their heads so that their hands held the canopy over the bed.

It was actually kind of clever, but again, he didn't think Lockett would appreciate it.

"What did you find?" she called out from the other side.

"A water bed. Looks comfy."

"Wait till you see this." She came tromping over his way, already pulling a nightgown and a fistful of supplies out of her plastic trash bag. "The bathroom is over here, behind a set of those white sheets they're using for drapes. It's really cool. Venus on the half shell, you know? The naked women with all the hair? And the shell she's standing in is the tub! There are these little fish at her feet for faucets, and more shells for the sink and toilet."

"Lockett, you sound like you like this."

"I do. It's kind of cute."

She smiled at him, with all the sunny, unconcerned, effervescent charm she'd had when she was seventeen. It had been a long time since he'd seen that smile.

He felt a definite pang in his heart, and he hardened himself against it. "What happened?"

She feigned innocence. "What do you mean?"

"I mean, what happened to you? Five seconds ago you were doing the usual whine and complain routine. Now you're acting like Miss Congeniality." He wrapped an arm around the closest naked lady column, leaning on it for support. "So what happened between then and now?"

"Well, you know, I'm trying to impress you." She smiled, dancing up the steps to the bed. "I know I've been unpleasant, and I decided it was time to shape up."

"Uh-huh," he said cynically.

"Why not?" She took the post opposite him, weaving around it lazily. "Things are looking up. We've got a whole lot more information, and we know we're closing in on whatever it is Stanford and my dad are up to."

"Don't forget—the search for us is escalating, too."

She shrugged, completely unconcerned. "They won't find us here. You were right about that—my father would never, ever think of looking for me in a place like this. I can hear him now. 'Cross that one off the list. My daughter would rather die than set foot in anything referred to as a Honeymoon Haven,'" she mimicked in a very snooty, nasal tone. "'But did you try the Ritz-Carlton?'"

"Well, at least I'm glad you're happy about this."

"Oh, come on, Ryan. Lighten up." Lockett grinned, swinging on her post like a maypole. "We've got the stuff to nail them. All we need to do is plow through the papers we stole from his safe. I'll take a shower and change into my own nightgown... Having my own clothes is a really welcome development, let me tell you. And then we'll sit here on our comfy water bed and spread the stuff out. Once we have our ducks in a row, we call the cops."

This was a switch. So much of a change that he was having a hard time buying it. "So now you think he did do something illegal?"

"Even if he didn't do anything wrong financially," she said softly, "I think there's a law against keeping your daughter a prisoner, against telling the FBI there's been a kidnapping when there hasn't, and..." She looked down at her feet. "And maybe against forging letters from your son-in-law to make your daughter think he betrayed her."

Ryan went very still. "What exactly do you mean?"

"You were in school then, at N.Y.U., do you remember?" Lockett darted onto the bed, wobbling as she tried to walk on water. "I was at home by myself a lot, doing absolutely nothing."

But she still wouldn't meet his eyes. What was going on here? She'd issued a moratorium on discussing this, and then brought it up herself. Would he ever understand her?

"I remember how things were," he said carefully.

She laughed. "Go ahead, say it. Terrible—that's how things were. We were both very young and very stupid, and we didn't know what to do once the initial melodrama faded. The princess was liberated from her tower, Prince Charming asked for her hand, and then what? That's the part the fairy tales never tell you."

Even though she was the one who'd set the guidelines for what was taboo, he found himself not wanting to rehash this, either. He wondered idly if there was anything to drink in the Temple of Venus. Could he go looking behind the curtains for a cache of Scotch?

"I hated the way we lived," she said simply.

There was a pause. "That was pretty obvious."

"Okay, so I admit it. I was a spoiled princess, and I hated being poor. I hated not having any of the things I was used to."

All he could offer her was a twisted smile. "Did you think I couldn't tell?"

"Oh, I knew you could tell." Finally, Lockett looked at him. Her eyes were blue and guileless, as if she were spilling out the unvarnished truth. "That was the problem. I was unhappy and I couldn't hide it, and you were absolutely miserable."

"I couldn't give you any of the things you were used to," he echoed.

"I know." She lifted her shoulders in a shrug, but his eyes traced the rise and fall of her breasts, molded so clearly by the top she wore. He forced his gaze back to her face. No good looking at what he couldn't touch.

"I could've lived with that," she told him. "But I couldn't live with you. You were moody, you were unreasonable, and you were playing a dangerous game with Max Fiorin." Lockett shook her head. "I hated that, you know. I hated waiting home by myself, wondering if you were still alive, or if somebody shot you when they were aiming for Max."

"I was never in any danger," he murmured.

"Yes, you were. Besides, it was illegal. And we both knew it."

"So you left me because of Max?"

"No." She met his gaze. "I left you because of you. The moods—the absences—all those things that were so romantic before we got married were impossible to live with after."

"So you left because I was impossible to live with?" he asked.

"No, actually, I never would've left just because of that." Her voice dropped into a huskier, softer register. "I would've fought for you, Tony. I would've stayed forever."

She'd called him Tony, and for a moment he felt like the boy he used to be. It went straight to his heart. "Why didn't you?"

"Because he had proof." She sank down onto the water bed, dropping her chin into her hands. Her words came more quickly, tumbling over each other as she rushed to get rid of them. "He found me in that awful apartment, and I was so ashamed that he saw where I was living. He said that he always knew you were no good, and look, here was the proof."

"What proof?"

Still gazing down, Lockett fooled with the fringe around the hem of her skirt. "Letters. In your handwriting. Big as life. Those letters definitely looked like they were from you. You had written that the marriage wasn't going anywhere, and you needed money." Bitter, mocking, she finished, "You said that you would be happy to return me, only slightly used, for half a million dollars, cash."

"I never wrote that, Lockett. You have to know I would never have said that."

"I know." Lockett looked drawn and pale. She shoved a strand of golden hair behind her ear, and she rolled over onto her stomach, staring away from him. "It's funny, because the past few days have proven that to me. Part of it is just waking up to what my father was and is capable of. It's a very hard lesson to learn."

"Are you okay with that?"

"Really?" She shook her head. "No. I'm not sure I ever will be. It's funny, because I got used to the idea a long time ago that he didn't really love me, not the way the dads on TV loved their daughters. But I thought he was proud of me . . . I thought there was this tiny corner of love.''

''Lockett, I'm sorry.''

''No,'' she said quickly. ''I'm not going to think about it. I'm going to freeze that. I don't want to feel it.''

This was awful. He'd wanted to wake Lockett up to the truth about her father, but he hadn't wanted to hurt her. Not like this.

''So now I know what he's capable of,'' she mused. ''And what you're not.''

She spoke so softly he could barely hear her. ''I thought I knew you so well then, and yet I believed it. Now, seeing you again, being with you, I thought I didn't know you at all. And yet I'm sure. You never would've written that. Not at all your style.''

As she sprawled below him on the water bed, he was getting a terrific view of her round little bottom in that frisky skirt, and he was having trouble remembering what they were talking about. The conversation they should've had years ago was finally here, and all he could think about was the thin, visible line of her black panties under that skirt, and the creamy curve of her sweet bottom.

This discussion was too important to lose track of because he couldn't keep his mind off the ache to have her. Now.

She sent him a quick glance over one shoulder. ''No, it was never your style.''

''Better late than never to figure that out,'' he mumbled.

God help him, all he could think about was how easy it would be to push her down into the bed, to peel off those tiny panties, to plunge himself inside with immediate release.

Ryan's whole body went rigid.

"Tony? What's wrong?"

She'd called him that again. But *Tony* had the right, and the permission, to make love to his wife whenever he wanted.

Ryan was another person entirely. "Look, I think you should stop calling me that. I haven't been Tony for a long time, okay?"

He turned, dying to leave, to stop his blood from pounding, his pulse from jumping. But there was nowhere to go, not even a door to hide behind.

"I think I'm going to, uh, take a shower." He practically leapt down into the main area and across to the curtains that hid the bathroom.

A cold shower would do him a world of good.

LOCKETT WAS SO CAUGHT UP in memories of the past that she had no idea why he had suddenly bolted like that. She thought they were finally on the right track, hashing it out, and suddenly he was gone.

He pulled back the drapes as he stormed into the Venus bathroom, and then just as quickly yanked them back into place.

As she flipped over and relaxed into the water bed, brooding, Lockett's gaze stayed fixed on the floating white veils across the room. What in the world was going on?

But there was no time to ponder. She heard the sound of rushing water—the shower, no doubt. Naked Venus was just a mural on the wall above the curvy pink shell of the tub, but Lockett's imagination fed Ryan into that picture. So bare and beautiful, so strong, coming face to face with Venus herself.

And then she saw the unbelievable. It wasn't her imagination. It was real.

He had turned on the light above the shower as he'd stepped in, illuminating the whole soft, peachy shell from within. Lockett swallowed around a lump in her throat, half rising from the bed. Clearly he didn't realize that the thin curtains had become translucent in the light, that she could see right through.

He was in profile. The long, lean lines of his body stretched up to meet the heady flow of water. His hair streamed black and glossy behind him, and his face tipped up, eyes closed, as he took the full brunt of the water.

Her gaze drifted down, inevitably, irresistibly. Powerful arms, flat stomach. Tanned, sinewy thighs and calves.

And in between . . .

Lockett tried to remember to breathe.

But her eyes were fastened there. No matter how hard she tried, she couldn't look away.

He was all man. He was magnificent.

Chapter Twelve

The Ecstasy Express

Any minute now, he was going to turn. He was going to look right through the curtain, and see her.

He was going to know that she was no better than a Peeping Tom, gaping at him from across the room. The thought of being caught should've made her run away. But she didn't move. She couldn't look away.

He lathered himself, skimming the hard planes and angles she found so tantalizing. He washed his hair, scrubbed himself mercilessly, and then just stood there, his eyes closed under the spray, letting it pummel him, letting the water sluice over him.

Lockett was dying.

She slipped down farther into the undulating bed. Her skin glazed with moist sweat and her nipples puckered and hardened under the skimpy top. She was on fire, wilting, suffocating, and he hadn't even touched her.

And then he shut off the shower . . . and turned.

He saw her.

She jumped up off the bed so fast it really did make her head spin.

"Lockett!" he shouted, but she didn't stop.

She ran all the way to the front door before she realized she had nowhere to go.

She leaned her head into the cool white wood of the door. She could feel him behind her. If she opened her eyes, she would see his bare feet, with water droplets still clinging to them, on the tile behind her.

"It wasn't my fault."

"Did you enjoy the view?" he asked in a low, dangerous tone. He knew damn well she had.

Slowly she turned back to him. She swallowed past a dry throat. "I—I wasn't trying to... It wasn't my fault. The light came on and you were there."

She barely noticed he had slung a towel around his hips. Talk about shutting the barn door after the horse had long since escaped. This particular stallion had already run for the hills and started a stampede.

She was shaking with the effort to control herself, to keep her greedy hands from reaching out to grab his shoulders, smoothing back his dripping hair, digging into his wet, slick skin.

"We've already broken all the rules but one," he said steadily, branding her with the heat in those intense, beautiful, moody emerald eyes. "I called you a princess, you brought up my money and uncle, and we've raked up the coals of our past till there's nothing left but ash. All that leaves is one last taboo."

Her own voice echoed in her ears. *Nobody is sleeping with anybody...*

"Want to break that one, too?" he whispered.

Oh, God, she was dying to.

But she mumbled, "I can't."

He pushed forward. She could feel him under the towel, all of him, nudging her. His arms framed her, trapped her against the door, and his head bent down closer.

He nipped her lips with a kiss, just a tiny, teasing kiss, as if it were a promise. Or maybe a dare.

"Why not, Lockett?"

"I don't know." Miserable, she realized she really didn't know. But she had to make him—and herself—understand what was holding her back. "It's just that... I was supposed to marry somebody else. I'm not the type of person who takes that commitment lightly, yet I almost wed someone I didn't love, someone I'm not even sure I knew all that well. I need to be careful now. I don't want to do the wrong thing again."

"Why are you so sure this is the wrong thing?" he asked softly. He leaned in and kissed her again, deeper, harder this time.

She was melting from the inside out. Her toes curled into the cold tile. "I'm not sure. Don't you see? That's just it. Being so close to you is very...confusing. I'm just not sure."

He slammed a hand into the door, startling them both. They both knew that she wouldn't have held out much longer, not if he'd kept up the sensual assault.

But they also both knew that plain old sensuality wasn't good enough anymore. Oh, sure, it would've felt great to work out a few of their kinks, blow their tension away in one fabulous session of lovemaking. But it wouldn't solve anything. This time, their minds had to be involved, too.

Ryan broke away, muttering an oath. "Damn it, Lockett," he said with considerable heat. "I've tried to stay away. I keep telling myself that you just about destroyed me the last time, because you didn't have enough trust or faith, and that I wouldn't get involved with you a second time. But here I am again, begging you, and you're not sure. *Begging.* The hell with it.''

''It wasn't just my fault. You didn't trust me, either,'' she cried. ''You thought the money was more important to me than you were, and you just sat there, waiting for me to leave. Well, okay, so I fulfilled your prophecy. But what was I going to do, when you obviously didn't believe in me?''

''This isn't getting us anywhere.'' He stalked away, his hair flicking wet drops as he ran a hand through it.

''It never does.''

''Take your shower. We were going to go over the files we stole, remember?''

Lockett sagged back against the door. Her heart was hammering, and her body still felt sticky, unstable. A shower was a good idea. They needed to unscramble the puzzle of her canceled wedding first, to rid themselves of demons like her father and former fiancé, before they turned their attention to what was going on between them.

What were they going to do about them? Whatever they did, it was going to have to wait.

Lockett grabbed a thick white robe out of the trash bag her sister had packed, and she headed for the Venus Rising Shower.

She planned to shower in the dark.

''ALL RIGHT. What have you got?'' Ryan shuffled a pile of papers. ''I've got the Seaboard Development file. This looks like a big loser, so that fills in one part of the equation, anyway. Your father lost money on Seaboard, and needed to get it from somewhere else to pay it back.''

They'd ordered room service, spread food and papers and themselves out on the big water bed, and so far they had managed to keep a respectable distance.

Lockett looked up. "Well, this blows your theory on my trust fund. There's hardly any money in it." She brandished one particular sheet of legal-size paper. "Yes, I am supposed to come into control of it once I marry, but it isn't much to brag about."

"What do you mean?"

"The money had dwindled down to practically nothing—a few hundred thousand." She shook her head, totally confused. So what else is new? "It's weird that there's so little. I mean, I would've thought it would be about three million, but it's gone down dramatically over the past two years. I really don't think my dad would've engineered a wedding to get his hands on it— there's just not enough there to help him out."

"All right." Ryan leaned back, chewing his lip. "So it's not to get at your money. But what about... Okay, what if, instead, he was desperate to hide the fact that the money was gone?"

Lockett narrowed her eyes, trying to absorb his new theory. "So he's misappropriated the money in my trust fund, and he's afraid I'll find out once I marry and take control of it?" Leaning in closer, she shook her head. "No, it just won't wash. He's trying to get me married, remember? He'd want me to stay single that way. Forever, if possible."

Ryan pitched backward, covering his eyes with one hand. "So what does that leave us? Nothing?"

"That leaves us with a big deal that apparently went very bad, and a trust fund that can't begin to cover the losses." She grabbed for his folder. "What did you say that was again? Seaboard Development. Funny, I've never heard of it. This is big money. This deal supposedly lost a bundle, lots more than my father would have had to invest of his own money, yet I've never heard of it."

"Is that unusual?"

"Well, yes. I mean, all of the Kensington finances are tied together. Daddy's company handles all of them. We get stock reports, profit and loss statements, all that kind of thing." She frowned. "I should really have heard of anything with this substantial an investment of family funds. And here's another funny thing. There are no annual reports in here, no letters to stockholders... For that matter, there's not even an address."

Next to her, Ryan sat up abruptly, causing a minor tidal wave in the bed. "Are you thinking what I'm thinking?"

Her eyes flashed to his. "I think so. Seaboard Development is a fake."

"Exactly."

"Or maybe not a fake. But a front. A place he can stick assets he isn't supposed to have. I can't believe it, but this is really starting to make sense to me." She began to get more excited, speaking quickly. "Say, for example, he takes clients' money that isn't supposed to be touched, and he puts it in his personal accounts and plays around. Only instead of making enough money to put their money back and pocket the profits, he loses. Big time. How to cover his tracks? Take it out of my trust fund. He manages it. No one ever checks there. But he also uses most of my money, too."

"And he needs more."

"But where does he get it?" She pounded the water bed with her fist, but the impact was too wobbly to do her any good. "We still don't know what happens next."

"You really don't think he'd get it from Stanford? Even for you?"

"No, not really." Pushing her hair back from her face, Lockett let out a long breath of frustration. "For one thing, I know Stanford doesn't have that kind of money. And for another, I don't think he'd pay it just to get me." She remembered his reaction when she'd told him she slept with another man. "He's in it for money, not for me."

"So we're back at square one."

"No, not really," she said again. "We can turn what we have over to the authorities. That should be enough to convince them that we're telling the truth. I mean, the depletion in my trust fund ought to tell them something."

"You would do that? Knowing that it might mean your father goes to jail?"

Lockett stared at a hole in the floor. She was trying very hard not to think about her father as a person, as the man she had always hoped he would be. She guessed, in a way, she'd hoped so hard for so long, she had actually convinced herself that he was the father she wanted him to be.

But when she looked back at his role in her life, she had to admit that he had not been. And it hurt. She knew it would hurt for a long time. The only thing she could do was freeze off that part of her heart. She had to pretend that he was not her father. He was just some other person named Elliot Kensington, someone she didn't know.

It was the only way she knew to deal with the disillusionment and the anger that kept nibbling at her.

My father lied to me for years. My father stole Ryan from me, twice. My father never loved me . . .

"I don't care if he goes to jail." She kept herself cool and collected. "What difference does it make?"

"If you're sure." But he took her arm, and he held her close for just a moment. "Let's not worry about it for right now, okay? We can't turn in what we have yet, anyway, because there's not enough to prove anything. And your father has enough influence to turn it all around against us. Trust me, Lockett, the authorities are not on our side."

"But we could—"

He kissed her quickly. "It's really late. Let's get some sleep, okay? We can talk about it in the morning."

But Lockett sat there on her side of the giant bed, turning it over in her mind. *Your father has enough influence to turn it all around against us . . .* She frowned. But did he? Or was Ryan just trying to protect her by not spilling everything to the authorities?

"The only thing left to do is go public," she whispered.

"Hmm?"

"Nothing."

But if Ryan was only sitting on the information to protect her, mistakenly thinking that it would upset her to see her father jailed, then maybe she could show him that he was wrong.

Maybe she didn't want to be protected. Maybe she wanted her father to pay for what he did.

Ryan slept on, unaware that Lockett's mind was racing.

SHE AWOKE to the sound of Ryan's voice. He was sitting on the pillows near the hot tub, speaking into the phone. He forbade her to make calls, but it was okay for him. How very interesting.

"Okay," she heard him mumble into the receiver. "Okay. Thanks for the info. I'll talk to you later."

And then he hung up.

"Who was that?" she called.

"Oh, nobody important." He rose. He was back in his trademark black T-shirt and jeans, and he looked great. The chauffeur thing was cute, but this was devastating. "Listen, I have to go out for a while, okay?" He smiled. "Don't get into any trouble while I'm gone."

And without another word, he walked out the door.

"Well, that's a fine how-do-you-do." Lockett got up, too, pondering Ryan's rather high-handed attitude as she dressed. She could think of lots of words to describe him.

"Insufferable, macho, controlling and overbearing" came to mind pretty fast.

Meanwhile, she had decided to be somewhat high-handed herself. Now that he had conveniently left the premises for a while, it was her chance to go forward with her plan. Even if Ryan was right, and sharing their information and their theory with the police wouldn't help their situation, she didn't see how it could hurt. And surely there was one newspaper with enough integrity, or a sharp enough nose for a story, to print *her* side of the story.

She grabbed a few important sheets of paper out of the trust fund file, and then she headed for the front desk with a definite sense of purpose.

"Do you have a copy machine?" she asked the clerk.

"Sure." There was a pause. "Do you want to use it?"

"Yes, I do." She smiled encouragingly. "I could also use some paper and some envelopes, if you have anything like that around."

"Okay. No problem." The girl motioned for Lockett to come around the back, into the hub of the reservations operation for the Honeymoon Haven. "The reservations girl is out to lunch, so you can use whatever you want."

"Thanks," Lockett offered, but she was already settling down to work.

A few minutes later she had copies of a few relevant pages, as well as a letter written out carefully in her own handwriting. The gist of it was that she was not a kidnap victim and that Ryan was only an innocent bystander. She also hinted rather strongly that her father and Stanford were hiding something, and that attached documents were part of the story.

Although most of the envelopes in the reservations area were clearly marked with the Honeymoon Haven return address, there were a few blank ones, and Lockett quickly gathered those up. She addressed one to the Chicago *Tribune* and one to the *Sun-Times*, with a third directed to the Chicago police department.

That left her with one envelope. The governor? One of her senators? Or maybe the FBI? She'd met the governor before, and she seemed like a nice, honest woman, so she chose that one for her last envelope.

She didn't have addresses, but she figured her recipients were well-known enough that it didn't matter.

Now all she needed was stamps. She felt guilty stealing them from the nice little stamp caddy on the reservations clerk's desk, but she didn't have any money. And they were right there, in plain sight. Lockett promised to try to remember to send a dollar to the reservations area at some later date.

Her letters were ready to go. Now she just needed somewhere to mail them from, where no one would see the postmark.

"Hello again," she said to the clerk.

"Hi. Did you need something else?"

"Well, yes. Do you live around here?"

"Me?" The girl looked confused. "Well, kind of. I live over the border in Illinois, but close."

Lockett hoped the difference in states would be confusing enough. "Could you do me a favor and mail these letters for me when you go home tonight?"

"Mail them from home?" she asked doubtfully. "Like, why?"

"It's important," Lockett answered. "I can't tell you why." With a sudden burst of inspiration, she said, "Kind of a practical joke."

"Oh, a joke." The clerk brightened. "Sure. Why not?"

"Great. Just remember—mail them when you get home, okay?"

"Sure."

She wondered whether she was leaving her precious missives in the care of someone who was too young and not nearly bright enough to handle things properly, but she didn't have any choice. It was either that or hitch a ride to Michigan to mail them from yet another state.

Feeling a bit apprehensive, but certain she'd done all she could, Lockett tripped back to the Temple of Venus.

She hadn't even had time to take her shoes off when the phone rang. Her sister again? Or Ryan. Maybe whoever it was Ryan was talking to earlier that morning.

She picked it up.

"Hello?"

"Lockett, is that you?"

"Charlie? How did you know I was here? Don't tell me you have automatic call-back, too?"

"My phone automatically stores all its calls," he said quickly. "I just tapped in and asked for all the numbers from the day you called. I couldn't believe it when I got the Honeymoon Haven Hotel. What are you doing *there?*"

Obviously, technology was running way ahead of Lockett. Who knew phones had all these splashy options?

"Listen, this is important," Charlie whispered. "Don't say anything, but they know where you are. Get out of there, now!"

"What? How? How do you know?"

"I volunteered to man the phones on the search committee," he whispered frantically. "I thought it would let me in on whatever popped, and I might be able to do you some good. I'm here right now. We've had two reports in the last half hour that people spotted the motorcycle in Indiana, plus another one from somebody who thought she saw a woman who looked like you in the lobby of a hotel called the Honeymoon Haven about ten minutes ago."

Lockett winced. One simple trip to the lobby and she'd been spotted. It was small consolation that Ryan and his bike had been even more conspicuous.

Charlie went on. "I checked against the number my machine stored when you called me, and bingo—same area code as the Honeymoon Haven in Indiana. They're closing in, Lockett. If they haven't found you already, it's just a matter of time.''

Ryan was gone. She didn't even have any way to leave. "What am I going to do?"

"Lockett, what are you doing at something called the Honeymoon Haven?"

"It's a long story."

"Well, I don't have time for that, and neither do you. The cops are going to be here any minute, and they've probably already got their little blue friends in Indiana coming after you, too. They've even ID'd the bike. They got a tip that the two of you were spotted in the Loop on a Ducati. Beautiful bike. I wish I had one. But, Lockett, the man could've picked something a little less conspicuous than a handmade Italian motorcycle."

She had been riding on the thing for days, and she had no idea what kind it was. "Are you sure?" That didn't sound like Ryan's taste.

"Forget about the bike. Get out of there!" he ordered. "And ditch the motorcycle as soon as you can."

"But I just sent out a pile of letters to tell people I wasn't kidnapped. As soon as they get my letters, we won't be fugitives anymore."

She could hear Charlie's sigh. "Listen, sweetie, I hate to burst your bubble, but they aren't going to believe you. They'll find you and throw your boyfriend in jail and ask questions later." He sighed again. "Your daddy has them snowed but good. Lockett, go now, okay? Don't wait around."

And the phone went dead in her hand.

"'Bye, Charlie," she whispered.

But goodbyes could wait. Right now she had to get out of there before the police came storming into the Temple of Venus.

It only took a few seconds to stash all the papers and her belongings into the trash bag. She was beginning to think this sort of luggage was much more useful than Louis Vuitton.

With her stuffed satchel on her back, she took off through Lover's Lagoon. She had only passed the first tiki torch when she thought she heard footsteps crunching on the path behind her.

Just some anonymous lover ready to partake of the lagoon's waters? Or someone more sinister?

The footfalls were loud, so it couldn't be bare feet. Who would go to the lagoon in shoes?

She turned in at the first tide pool, scrambling over grass and vines, plastering herself up against a big rock, listening for sounds of pursuit. She heard the footsteps stop, and then pad more softly, as they, too, climbed into the jungle.

She pressed on, winding farther into the heart of Lover's Lagoon. This was worse than a real jungle, and her hefty bag was making a quiet escape impossible.

"Excuse me," she whispered as she charged right into a private scene in a little inlet with a waterfall. "So sorry."

She averted her eyes and crashed on, under a tree, around a big rock, through another inlet, and finally out into a kind of clearing. She slowed. Which way should she go?

But as she hesitated, the hairs on the nape of her neck began to prickle.

A hand grabbed her shoulder.

Whirling, she lashed out with her garbage bag, knocking him down as she prepared to leap over him. But then she saw long, dark hair, black T-shirt and jeans.

"Ryan!" She collapsed next to him with relief. "It was *you* following me. I thought it was the police. I thought it was the bad guys."

"Why?" he gasped, holding his middle where she'd walloped him with the bag.

Helping him to his feet, leading them both out of Lover's Lagoon, Lockett started with, "Don't get all upset, but we have to get out of here as quickly as we can."

A long pause held him. "Are you going to tell me why?"

"There's no good way to put this." She clutched his hand and dragged him to his feet. "My friend Charlie called. He's been manning some kind of tip line or something. The motorcycle was spotted, plus somebody saw me in the lobby here and called the cops. So they know where we are, and Charlie thinks they'll be here soon."

"Well, we knew they'd find us sooner or later." Ryan reached for her bag, already taking over to guide her out of the lagoon. "I was just hoping it would be later."

"Me, too."

RYAN REFUSED to ditch the motorcycle, although she told him several times she really thought it was a good idea. She was getting the idea that bike was his baby. He also wouldn't let her bring the garbage bag with all her possessions with her. Instead he told her to choose a few important things, and to leave the rest tied to the bike. Then he parked it in a commuter lot, made a quick phone call to parts unknown, and hustled her onto the next train to the city.

At Union Station, in the middle of downtown Chicago, with cops swarming everywhere, the two of them walked brazenly right through and hopped on a train headed south by southwest.

Safe in her sunglasses and baseball hat, Lockett tried not to act suspicious until they were safely on the train. Tickets in hand, they trudged wearily into their tiny sleeping compartment.

"Where are we going?" Lockett asked. She just wanted to pull down the teensy-weensy bed and climb in. She was exhausted.

No wonder. She kept having to share beds with Ryan, which was not the best way to get any sleep. For right now, she contented herself by curling up on the bench seat and pillowing her head on one arm.

"Chicago," Ryan told her. He cracked the blinds and peered out the window at the rather dull scenery flashing past.

"Ryan, we're heading away from Chicago," she said patiently.

"I know."

"I'm sorry. I'm confused. I thought you said we were heading *for* Chicago."

"We are."

"How can we head away from there and get there at the same time?"

"Don't worry," he said kindly. He reached over to pat her hand. "It's confusing on purpose. Your old man and your boyfriend, they know we don't have enough evidence to figure them out yet, right?"

"I guess so." What in the world did that have to do with trains?

"So they're going to assume we'll be hiding somewhere in Chicago, ready to swoop out and break into some more safes, looking for evidence."

"But we're not," she said logically. "We just got tickets to Kansas City."

"But we're not getting off in Kansas City."

"We're not?"

"No." Ryan leaned away, flapped the blinds back down, and turned to her. "We should hit Kansas City sometime in the middle of the night. But we're going to stay on the train. We're going to turn right around and go back to Chicago."

"We're going to Kansas City for five minutes, and then turn around and come back?"

Ryan shrugged, maddeningly calm. It was as if he enjoyed being on the run; it was standing still that made him uneasy.

"We couldn't do anything tonight, anyway. I put out some feelers, but I have to wait until tomorrow to see what comes up." He yawned. "So we needed a place to crash."

"And this is it, hmm?"

"Tell me, Lockett, do you think they'll look for us on a train going to Kansas City and heading right back?" He offered her an easy smile. "It seemed to me a moving motel was the best place to get some sleep, with the least chance of getting caught."

"What kind of feelers did you put out?" she inquired. "And who did you call from the commuter station?"

"Does it matter?"

"Well, yes. I'm a part of this team, too. I have a right to know what's going on," she insisted.

"You're better off not knowing." His green eyes grew even darker, more difficult to read. "It's safer that way."

"What are you up to, Ryan? I really don't like being kept in the dark." Lockett gazed at Ryan for a long moment. What kind of informant would be safer if kept quiet? "What is this all about?"

"Lockett," he began, as if he didn't know quite how to approach this. "Look, I've been in contact with Uncle Max, okay? I know the mere mention of his name trips all your switches. But I need him to crack this."

"Oh, Ryan..." Lockett leaned her head back against the rest. "It's not that I hate him for what he is, although a lot of people do. It's that I dislike what he does to you. You could be so much more, if you could just get out from under his control."

"He doesn't control me," he said flatly.

"He's dangerous," she persisted. "The best thing— your only resource—is to steer clear of him. You got arrested because of him, remember? Your father died because of him. Ryan, he is an evil man."

"Lockett, you've never even met him."

"Who needs to meet him?" Lockett sighed. "The man's bad points have been a matter of public record for years. I mean, he'd probably be in prison right now if half the witnesses hadn't disappeared before they could get him to trial the last time."

"He is what he is. And part of what he is is my uncle." Restless, Ryan drew the blinds completely, peering out at the cornfields and flat farmsteads of Illinois. As far as Lockett was concerned, there wasn't much to look at out there. But he kept gazing out there, nonetheless. "Your family isn't exactly coming up roses at the moment."

"That doesn't change it, Ryan. This isn't a competition for who has the worst relatives," she told him.

"The world isn't always black and white, Lockett. Sometimes you have to see the shades of gray."

"Like rich and poor?" She pressed her point, hoisting him with his own petard. "Yes, Tony, that's right. You always gave me such a hard time for being born with a silver spoon in my mouth. In your mind, the common man could do no wrong, and people like my father could do no right. But maybe sometimes poor people can be just as greedy and venal as the rich ones."

"Touché."

"Glad we got that settled."

"We can settle pretty much anything you want, princess." He paced off the distance in the tiny compartment. "We've got all night."

"Don't call me princess."

"Don't call me Tony."

It was a draw. Neither spoke for several minutes, until they looked at each other and, out of the blue, they both smiled.

"Do we have to wait for a porter? Or can you draw my bunk now?" Lockett asked him. "I'm really exhausted. I think I'd like to take a nap. Maybe I'll just sleep through Kansas City and back. I've always had a fantasy about speeding through the night on a train. Kind of romantic. *Strangers on a Train* or something."

"*Strangers on a Train* was a murder mystery," he said dryly. "But don't let me put a damper on your fantasy. Which one do you want? Top or bottom?"

"Bottom." She yawned. "I might fall out if I was up there."

"That's okay. I always did prefer to be on top," he returned. And then he pulled out his penknife and unlatched both bunks, swinging them into place.

The reality of a train bunk wasn't as romantic as her fantasy, but she was tired enough to try it out, anyway. After hunting through all the compartments in the car, Lockett found a pillow. She started to climb into bed, not bothering to look for a nightgown or even to brush her teeth.

"Good night, Ryan," she said drowsily.

"Good night, Lockett. Sleep tight," he whispered.

And then all she heard was the sound of the rails singing through the night.

Chapter Thirteen

Lake L'Amour

The train chugged along into the night. There was something soothing about the rhythm of the rails, but Lockett couldn't sleep.

Finally, she had her own bed, such as it was. So why couldn't she fall asleep?

"Tony," she whispered. "Are you awake up there?"

"Lockett..." His voice was soft, a shade raspy. "I asked you not to call me that. It brings up things I'd rather not remember."

"I'm sorry. I don't mean to. It just slips out every once in a while without warning. I mean, most of the time you're Ryan to me—the secretive, arrogant, impenetrable man in black." She smiled into the night. "But sometimes I see Tony. He's the beautiful one, the knight who saved me at the pool party. The one who blushed when I kissed him."

"He's gone, Lockett."

"Is he?"

"Yeah."

She could hear him shifting around him up there. "Where did he go?"

"He died, Lockett," Ryan said quietly. "He was very young and very naive. And when his wife left him, he couldn't make it."

His words cut her like a knife. She knew they were meant to. "I said I was sorry. I was young and stupid, too, okay?" Sitting up without warning, she smacked her head hard against the edge of his bunk.

"Did you hurt yourself?"

Oh, sure. Now he was solicitous and kind. After he'd wounded her to the quick by saying she'd *killed* him.

"I'm fine," she mumbled. "I just have a monstrous headache now."

A heavy silence hung between them.

"You didn't, you know," he said softly.

"Didn't what?"

"Say you were sorry. All this time, I thought you cut out because there wasn't enough money."

"Not a very attractive image of me."

Angrily he asked, "What else was I supposed to think?"

"We were both stupid." Holding her head, Lockett sighed. "Me more than you, I admit it. And if I haven't said it before, I will now. *I am sorry.* I thought it was all over. I thought you didn't want me anymore. I left. I should have done things differently, but I didn't. And it's all a long time ago."

"And where does that leave us?"

Somehow it was easier to talk now that she wasn't looking at him. She knew he was up there in the darkness, speeding to or from Kansas City, she wasn't sure which. She knew she could talk to him, say what she had to say, without seeing his face or his eyes. It was so much less complicated.

"I love you," she whispered. It was so faint she wasn't sure he would hear it. Maybe that was better.

"Don't say that if you don't mean it."

He had heard. Lockett's heart beat faster. She didn't hear any return confession from him.

But it didn't stop her. "I have always loved you," she said. "From the first moment I saw you digging a hole for a tree under my window. Back then, it was so easy. I must've told you I loved you a million times. And it was wonderful to be so sure. I still love you. I still feel like you're a part of my heart. But, Ryan, I don't know if that's enough anymore."

"I don't, either." His voice was still a little husky. It tickled her nerve endings. It made her want to close her eyes and let him wrap himself around her. "And I don't know if I still love you. I did. I loved you more than anything. But it hurt. And I don't ever want to hurt like that again."

"I know."

The train pushed on, the wheels beneath them sang against the metal rails, and silence once again fell in their small sleeping compartment.

"Lockett," he said, breaking the hush. "Why don't you come up here and sleep with me? Nothing we shouldn't do. Nothing we can't handle. I'll just hold you, and we'll both sleep better."

Trust. She had to trust his word that he wouldn't kiss her or tease her again, wouldn't start anything she couldn't control. She had to trust that they were on the same wavelength.

She was up there in a flash.

Snuggled in beside him, Lockett pressed her eyes closed. She drank in the scent of him, the leather and clean soap smell she had grown to recognize, and she angled a hand in the silken strands of his long, dark hair.

She smiled. She knew, if he didn't, that he still loved her.

"WHAT TIME IS IT?" she asked as he shook her awake. She felt like she'd been sleeping forever.

"It's morning. Get going, Lockett. We just have time for some breakfast before we pull back into Union Station."

Good grief. He sounded positively husbandlike. Up top, Lockett smiled. They might've just slept, but at least they'd managed to clear the air.

"Get moving."

"Okay, okay." It didn't take her long to complete her toilette—with no makeup, and most of her face covered behind the pieces of her disguise, it didn't really matter.

They managed to get a glass of orange juice and a sweet roll in the club car, and then they were primed and ready, all set to jump off the train as it screeched to a halt inside the terminal in Chicago.

Oddly enough, Lockett wasn't that anxious to leave. She had fond memories of curling up next to Ryan in that top bunk. And after several days of being on the run, of sleeping in stagecoaches and water beds, it was great to clock a good twelve hours of sleep.

But the clang of the train and the hustle and bustle of the station told them their idyll was over. Porters swarmed with luggage, everybody seemed to be in a hurry, and she and Ryan fell right into the line of departing passengers.

"Keep a low profile," he told her. "There are probably cops around."

Were there ever. Maybe she was just hypersensitive,
but everywhere she looked she saw blue uniforms. A
they did their best to blend into the crowd, marching
along out of the gate area with everyone else, Locket
caught a quick glimpse of a TV blasting from a nearby
snack bar.

It wasn't much of a look, but it was enough. *She wa*
on that television, or at least, her mug shot. She el
bowed Ryan, gesturing toward the lunch counter. "How
about a cup of coffee, darling?"

"Do you really think we have time for that, sweet
heart?"

"I think we should make time, darling." She edge
to the side, aiming for the snack bar, but almost col
lided with a large woman pushing a baby carriage.

"Hey, watch it," the woman snapped.

Lockett stopped in her tracks.

"What's your problem?" the man behind he
growled, slamming her hard with his suitcase.

"Ouch."

"Watch your luggage, buddy. Keep it away from my
wife," Ryan warned him.

"You shut up, mister. I didn't touch her. Although
somebody ought to tell her that we don't like then
Pacers in this town. Da Bulls rule here."

Lockett fingered her hat. She didn't know enough
about basketball to realize she was risking a social in
cident on the basis of the team she advertised.

At the sound of loud voices, a policeman entered th
fray. With a bored face, he inquired, "You guys got
problem?"

"No problem." Lockett smiled sweetly, grabbin
Ryan's arms. "My husband is just overprotective. Yo

know," she said, patting her flat tummy. "Expectant father."

"Uh-huh," the cop said in the same bland tone. "Move along."

"We'd be happy to." This time, under the jaded eye of the policeman, they made it successfully into the coffee shop.

"I saw myself on television," she whispered. "I wanted to know what they were saying about me. Maybe my letters got to the police by now. Maybe they believed me, and the search has been called off."

But her face was long gone by the time they angled up to the counter under the TV set. An attractive young woman with bouffant hair now dominated the screen, droning on about something, while a little box with the word "kidnap" graced the space above her shoulder.

"Could you turn that up, please?" Lockett requested as she scooted onto a stool.

"Sure, I got nothing better to do than turn up the damn TV." The man behind the counter, who was clearly not in the running for employee of the month, cranked it up a notch, slamming a scummy plastic menu down in front of her at the same time. "Whatcha want?"

"I haven't had time to look at it yet."

"Okay." And he shuffled away.

"You're not doing a very good job of blending in," Ryan commented.

"Neither are you. What was that about keeping his luggage away from your wife?" But then she heard her name coming from the TV. "Shh."

They both listened intently.

"The whereabouts of Lockett Kensington are still unknown at this time, although police say they continue to amass tips and clues in this baffling case. A sketch of her suspected kidnapper was released by police this morning.''

A hideous picture that thankfully looked very little like Ryan filled the screen.

''If you see this man, do not attempt to talk to him or capture him. He is considered armed and dangerous. Here,'' the woman went on, ''is the plaintive plea issued by the missing woman's fiancé just this morning.''

Oh, please. Just what she didn't need this early in the morning was to look at Stanford oozing with fake concern.

''We have reason to believe that Lockett has not only been kidnapped, but also that she may have—'' He broke off, but continued with a surface show of courage. ''We think she may have become unbalanced by the ordeal, or perhaps brainwashed, and that she may no longer realize how much we love her and want her to come home. Come home, Lockett, if you can. I love you, darling. It's not too late.''

''Let's leave before I lose my lunch,'' she muttered.

''You haven't eaten yet.''

''It doesn't matter. I'll lose *something* if I hear one more word out of his mouth.''

Arm in arm, they shuffled through the train station. Lockett was still fuming, even as she tried to look nonchalant.

''Did you hear that?'' she whispered. ''He said I was *brainwashed*. The Patty Hearst of the '90s. This is so insulting.''

''Calm down, will you? People are starting to stare.''

''We have to do something, and we have to do it right away. *Brainwashed*,'' she said again. ''I am not going to stand by and let them tell people I've been brain-washed. There has to be a way."

"No more letters, please?"

"So what do we do now?" she asked. "Back to the commuter station where we left the motorcycle?"

"There's supposed to be a car waiting for us," he told her, ushering her out the big doors and onto the street.

There was a car, all right. A long, black, funereal limousine.

A very impressive man, with shoulders the size of Soldier Field and a nose that had clearly been broken several times, hustled right up to them.

"Mr. Ryan," he said respectfully. If he'd had a cap, Lockett was sure he would've doffed it. "It's very nice to see you again, Mr. Ryan. And the lady, too. The boss said as how I should meet you, pick you up."

The boss? Lockett glanced at Ryan. What was this all about?

"Nice to see you, too, Louie." He clenched his jaw. "And where did Mr. Fiorin tell you to take us?"

Mr. Fiorin, huh? By the size of the car and the looks of the palooka with the nose, she should've guessed.

The man moved to open the back door of the limo. He motioned to Lockett to get in.

"Go ahead," Ryan said dryly. "I don't think we have a choice." As she quietly ducked into the car, Ryan turned back to the driver. "Okay, Louie, so where are we going?"

"To the lake house. Mr. Fiorin thinks maybe you're in a little trouble. Maybe you need his help."

Lockett swallowed, sinking into the thick leather seats of the stretch limo. It appeared she was going to meet a real godfather. This was a first.

NOBODY SAID A WORD as they rode out of the city. The windows were smoked, so she couldn't tell where they were headed. But Louie had mentioned a lake house. Could be in Illinois, of course, but Lockett got it fixed in her mind that they were going to Wisconsin.

She hoped it wasn't as far as Minnesota or something. Would Ryan's uncle scoop them up and carry them off for a ten-hour drive? She sent her ex-husband an alarmed glance, but he was preoccupied.

She would've paid a pretty penny to find out what he was thinking just then. After all, he knew Max Fiorin a lot better than she did, no matter how much she'd read in the papers.

Would this command appearance be on the pleasant side? *Ryan, my boy, you don't visit often enough. What can I do for you? Name it, it's yours. You want old Kensington out of the way? Marsh, too? No problem.*

Or maybe on the unpleasant side. *What do you think you're doing, getting mixed up with this crazy dame? She's no good for you— I told you years ago.*

Lockett shivered. Either of the imaginary dialogues was pretty ludicrous. She just hoped they all came out of this in one piece, with nobody sleeping with the fishes before dinner.

Her stomach rumbled at the idea of dinner. She hadn't had a decent meal in days. At least the chances seemed good that Ryan's uncle would feed them.

"Are you hungry, ma'am?" the driver inquired politely. He swung open a small refrigerator, filled with small containers of this and that, as well as two chilled bottles of extremely expensive champagne. "We will be arriving at Mr. Fiorin's house momentarily, so perhaps you would prefer to wait to see what he has prepared for his guests there. But if you would require a snack now, to tide you over, I can offer caviar, pâté, or shrimp. I regret I have nothing more substantial to offer a lady such as yourself."

"He heard your stomach growl," Ryan whispered. "He's being polite. Don't worry—it's not poisoned."

She gave him a swift elbow. She might not condone the less charming aspects of his uncle's business, but she certainly wasn't rude enough to mention poison in front of a henchman. "I'd, uh, love a cracker and some pâté," she said brightly.

"Champagne?" he offered.

"No, thank you. Although that certainly is a lovely vintage."

"Yes. Mr. Fiorin is quite particular on the subject of wine."

So far, Mr. Fiorin had a lot more in common with her father than he did with the fictional godfather Lockett had been expecting.

She nibbled her cracker as they sped on through the countryside. And before she knew it, the limo slowed and then stopped.

Louie was out first, with a protective hand inside his jacket. That caused her a moment of alarm. Was he going for his gun to protect them from someone? Or keep them in line?

Either way, it was very unsettling.

The doors of the limousine opened onto a restful, green, country setting, with birds chirping and leaves rustling and waves splashing on the shore of a private lake.

They were on a crushed-gravel drive circling in front of a tasteful, sprawling frame house done in natural wood tones. It was large enough to qualify as an estate, and posh enough to belong to any of her father's closest friends.

If she'd expected something garish or ostentatious, this wasn't it. The only false note was the high electrical fence running all around the compound. It looked like somebody was expecting heavy artillery.

"Mr. Ryan. Ma'am," the driver said, motioning toward the front door. A man in a starched black uniform was waiting to greet them.

"Very nice," Lockett murmured. Linking her arm through Ryan's, she wished she were wearing something better than a T-shirt and jeans for this visit to the country. Something in a nice linen suit would've felt more appropriate. Or even tennis whites.

Anything but this ghastly Indiana Pacers baseball hat. With that thought in mind, she released Ryan's arm long enough to pull off the hat and shake out her hair.

She had to catch herself. Why did she care what she wore to meet a criminal? Okay, so he was a relative of Ryan's. But he was still a gangster. She didn't have anything to prove.

"Miss Kensington," the butler offered in a clipped British accent. "Allow me to escort you to your room."

"Are we staying?" Lockett asked Ryan. "Overnight?"

"Looks that way, doesn't it?"

"This way, Miss Kensington," he said again.

But she hesitated. "Isn't Ryan coming?"

"Not just this second," Louie said apologetically. "The boss requires his presence."

"We're splitting up, then?" she asked nervously.

Ryan squeezed her hand. "Don't worry. It's just for a second. I'll come and get you as soon as I see my uncle and find out what he wants."

"Okay." And she allowed herself to be led away. But as she trailed down the endless hallway behind the very proper butler, she peeked over her shoulder once or twice. Ryan was getting smaller back there.

The house was perfectly lovely, and Lockett was escorted into a comfortable, understated room with a big picture window overlooking the lake. Its water was calm and blue, undisturbed by boats or swimmers at the moment. It was impossible to tell how many people were in residence here, but the intense stillness made her think they were pretty much alone. Just her and Ryan, a few servants, and Uncle Max.

"Cheery thought," she murmured to herself. "Maybe there used to be more, but they ended up in the bottom of the lake for using the wrong soup spoon."

Quickly she scanned the room for bugs or taping equipment, not that she would've known it if she'd seen it. But what if somebody'd heard her say that? She'd be the next one in the cement overshoes.

She waited several long minutes for the guards to come and haul her away for speaking out of turn, but nothing happened. So Lockett settled on the end of the bed, gazing out at the placid, unruffled lake, waiting to see what happened next.

Nothing. She expected someone to come and get her at any moment, to take her to wherever Ryan was.

Other than taking a nap or staring at the lake till her eyes crossed, she had nothing to do, either. Lockett was not one given to long bouts of solitude and meditation.

At first she paced. Then she sat some more. And then she paced some more.

Finally she got up, went to the door, and opened it. Nobody there. So what if this was the house of a Mafia don? She couldn't hang out in that room, twiddling her thumbs, forever. So she tromped right out in the hall. Nobody there, either.

Feeling brave, Lockett tried to retrace her steps the way she'd been led by the butler. But the halls were endless and they seemed to curve back around on themselves. She was sure she'd passed the same staircase three or four times. After several unsuccessful tries to navigate the place, she became sure she was lost.

Too bad she hadn't left a trail of bread crumbs. Her stomach growled. Too bad she didn't have any to eat.

Finally she thought she heard voices off to her left. She didn't care who it was at this point. She'd just have to throw herself on their mercy and admit she was wandering where she had no right to be.

The voices seemed to be coming from behind a rather impressive oak door. She bent down closer, sticking her ear to the door. No sense in being unprepared for whatever lay inside.

"You always were a difficult boy," a gruff, weary voice declared. "Here you are, in trouble again. That Kensington girl, she's no good for you— I told you years ago."

Lockett gulped. The voice of the godfather. And he was saying exactly what she'd predicted he would!

"I feel a certain responsibility for her safety," Ryan's voice responded. "In my heart, she's still my wife. I take my responsibilities seriously."

In my heart, she's still my wife... Lockett's breath caught in her throat. She leaned in closer.

"You take everything too seriously. That's your problem." The way he spoke, she could almost see the old man shaking his head at the folly of his godson. "So, listen. You got a problem. Why don't you come to me to make this problem go away? I can do that for you."

Lockett put a hand to her mouth. She'd predicted that, too.

But Ryan said, "I like to solve my problems myself."

"Ah, you always did. Too damn independent."

It was tricky business eavesdropping. You always risked hearing things you didn't want to hear. But so far, so good. He still thought of her as his wife. Sweet, wonderful, welcome news. And his uncle was mad at him for being independent, which was fine by her.

"Your father, he was my right hand. I have a special fondness in my heart for him. And this is why I look out for you."

He was playing all his high cards. Lockett knew very little about Ryan's father, but she did know he had been Max's right-hand man until he'd died in the line of fire. Invoking his name was probably how Max managed to keep Ryan in line.

"I appreciate your concern, Uncle Max. But I don't need your help."

"Bah!" Something heavy slammed inside the room. "You're doing so well without it? That's why your face is in the papers? They're saying you're connected. They're printing my name, and I don't like it."

"They say what they say. It doesn't bother me."

"So you refuse to come into my business all these years, and yet it doesn't bother you when the girl's father tells everyone you're in my pocket?" the old man asked shrewdly.

"They say what they say," Ryan repeated.

"So, okay. You don't want me to lean on anybody. I can respect that. But there must be some help I can offer you."

"Information," Ryan said slowly. "If you can give me the information I need, I will be grateful."

"This I cannot give you."

"I need to know what Lockett's father is protecting, Uncle Max. You told me he lost a lot of money. But how? And why did he want her to get married? How does this work?"

"I can't tell you."

There was a long pause. "Can't? Or won't?"

"Any way you want it."

Why would Ryan think his uncle would know things like that? She pressed her ear closer just as a dark, good-looking young man rounded the corner. Joey. He had this maddening habit of popping up in all the wrong places.

He spied her immediately, of course. Her ungainly position stuck out in the hall made that inevitable. Lockett jumped back, but it was too late. He had to know she'd been eavesdropping.

"Hi," he said cheerfully. "Hear anything good?"

"Of course not," she returned quickly. "I mean, that is, I didn't hear anything."

"Hello, again, Lockett. Long time no see."

Not long enough. Joey was okay, but she just found herself not liking him. Was it the fact that he was Max's son? Or just that he always had that smirky attitude?

"So, are you in on this meeting?" She indicated her thumb at the door.

"No, actually." He smiled. He really was very good-looking, in a slick kind of way. "There's a lot Max doesn't include me in."

She sensed there was a certain edge to that statement. "Surely as his son you're included in anything you want to be."

But Joey just shrugged. "I'm supposed to take over, someday. But who knows?" He gave her a conspiratorial nudge. "Just between you and me, I think he'd rather have Ryan as his heir apparent, but Ryan's never gone for the idea."

"Well, I certainly hope not!" She realized how that sounded and she backtracked in a hurry. "Not that I want to malign your, uh, chosen profession or anything, but I've always felt that Ryan should..." She broke off awkwardly.

"Steer clear? Yeah, he thinks so, too." He cocked a thumb at the door this time. "So, do you want to go in? Or should we stand in the hall all day?"

And that was how she became introduced to Max Fiorin, Chicago's most notorious gang boss in fifty years. Joey took her in and said, "Hey, Dad, this is Lockett, Ryan's wife. I brought her to meet you."

"Miss Kensington," the old man said courteously. "I am very pleased to meet you at last."

Not terribly tall, not terribly handsome, Max Fiorin was still very distinguished. There was something about him that did not brook disagreement. Again, she was struck by how well he would fit in her father's world. Cutthroats were cutthroats, it appeared, no matter what milieu they showed up in.

Any discussion of business ended as soon as she and Joey entered. After exchanging pleasantries, somebody mentioned something about dinner, and they all retired to the dining room.

The meal was huge and very prettily prepared, with noiseless servants wheeling courses in and out. Even her own privileged background had not prepared her for this sort of Edwardian repast.

But it was lovely.

The minutes slipped past easily. How odd to enjoy such a diverting evening in the company of crooks.

So far she'd had no opportunity to get Ryan alone, to tell him she'd heard the lovely things he'd said, and she very much appreciated the sentiment. She tried to waggle her eyebrows at him, to send him meaningful glances, but it didn't seem to get her anywhere.

Finally, after hours at the dinner table, Max signaled the servants that they were done.

"Someone will show you back to your room, Miss Kensington. I believe some clothing and other items have been laid out for you." He nodded, dismissing her. "Ryan, Joey, we'll have cigars."

Lockett did not appreciate being dismissed like that, just because she was female. No wonder Ryan was so pushy, so high-handed. He'd learned it at his uncle's knee.

"Excuse me? Ryan? Can I speak to you for a second?"

Under the disapproving gaze of his uncle, Ryan crossed to her. He murmured, "Look, I know you're dying to ream me out for bringing you here, but it will have to wait. I'll see you in the morning."

Morning? But what about tonight? She had decided she loved him. She had reconciled his position in the Fiorin clan, mulled over his uncle's statements, decided he was clean, and determined she could deal with his dubious connections. And last but certainly not least, she had heard him say that in his heart, she was his *wife*.

Now she was supposed to toddle off to bed and talk to him in the morning?

She had been toying with the idea of making love with him tonight! After all, what were they waiting for?

It wasn't as if they hadn't been lusting for each other ever since he'd shown up at the pool. Maybe she didn't want to wait one more night.

"Tomorrow," he said. "I'll give you all the opportunity you want to rake me over the coals."

He lined up with Max and Joey, while the butler hovered at Lockett's elbow, anxious to usher her out so the power elite could smoke their cigars in peace.

She had no choice but to leave. Tomorrow. Yes, she would have something to say to Antonio Ryan....

Chapter Fourteen

Love Among the Lace

There was a tap at Lockett's door. Thank goodness. Ryan hadn't wanted to wait till morning, either.

She jumped out of bed and threw open the door. "Darling..."

"Uh, I don't think so."

It was Joey. His tie was askew, his collar undone, and he smelled heavily of brandy and cigars.

"Look, I'm sorry to bother you so late." He glanced out in the hall and then back at her. "May I come in? This is important."

"Sure. I guess." Backing up, crossing her arms over the delicate white nightgown she was wearing, Lockett switched on a light.

In her borrowed sleeping attire, in the middle of the night, Lockett did her best to look dignified in front of Joey. What was he doing here, anyway?

"I figure you overheard pretty much of my father and Ryan's conversation earlier, the one where your ear was pressed to the door." A crooked smile curved his lips.

"Well, I caught some of it," she allowed.

"Yeah, I thought so. I got a rerun a little while ago. The thing is…" Joey stopped, but Lockett gave him her most encouraging look.

"Go on."

"The thing is, Max is never going to tell Ryan what he wants to hear. But I think Ryan already suspects."

"Suspects what?"

Joey eyed her shrewdly. "Max…is the one who gave Elliot Kensington the loan."

Lockett gasped, sitting down on the edge of the bed abruptly. "My father borrowed money from the mob?" Her head was spinning. That by itself was enough to ruin his reputation. No wonder he'd tried to cover it up. But what could have possessed him? "Oh, Daddy," she whispered, "you are in so much trouble." Glancing up at Joey, she asked, "How much did he borrow?"

"A couple million." Joey shoved his hands into his pockets. "I'd say your old man was in serious trouble. He had spent a lot of money—that wasn't his—on a very risky venture that he felt sure would bring in big bucks. It didn't."

"Seaboard Development," she said wearily.

"I don't know. I just know that he borrowed some very large sums from my father to keep the books better balanced." He gave her a more careful glance. "But then, of course, my father expected the money to be paid back…with substantial interest."

"Loan-sharking, I believe it's called," she said dryly.

"And the thing is, he hasn't repaid his debts. His accounts are in arrears, shall we say? Max is getting anxious to get his payments."

"What's going to happen?" she asked quickly. She might be disillusioned and angry at her father for all his double dealings, but she still wouldn't wish anything to happen to him. A respected businessman, a pillar of the community, laid so low. What was she going to do? This was all so horrifying.

"Your father made promises to pay—as soon as you got married."

"As soon as I—" She gulped. "I see." Ryan had been right all along. Something to do with her marriage to Stanford would've meant money for her father. "Joey, why are you telling me? Why not go to Ryan?"

"I thought..." Joey chewed his lip. "Look, I know Ryan has it in for your father. If I tell him, he takes this to the cops in no time flat. But I thought you should be the one to decide what happens. He's your father. It should be your call."

"But what you've told me..." Lockett glanced up at his tense face. "It implicates *your* father, as well. I know the police have been looking for evidence to send Max to jail for a very long time."

Joey said carefully, "I can't deny that."

"And by giving me this information, well, if I decide to turn in my father," Lockett mused, "it might very well topple Max as well. Joey, are you prepared for that?"

"Obviously." He backed toward the door. "I wouldn't have told you otherwise."

"Obviously." She swallowed. Here she was, in possession of important information, and she wished someone else would make a decision about what to do. Could she turn in her father? Or should she confront him with the evidence.

"Joey, I don't know what to do..."

But he was already gone. And he'd left a set of car keys on the dresser.

Why had he told her this, when he knew it would harm his father as well as hers? He said he was aware of the consequences. Maybe he *wanted* those consequences.

She would've liked to believe that Joey was having pangs of conscience at the nasty deeds his father had pulled. But she had a feeling she was in the middle of an explosive family problem. If Joey wanted to take over, what better way to peacefully topple the old man than to send him to prison?

If Lockett used Joey's information. But could she do that to her father?

"Oh, Ryan, where are you when I need you?" she asked miserably. This was more than she could decide on her own.

"Lockett?" someone whispered from the door.

"Good timing," she said fervently. And she ran into his arms.

"I guess you missed me." Ryan looked even more disheveled than Joey had. He was wearing a white dress shirt, rumpled and not tucked in, black jeans with the top snap undone, and no shoes. The scent of Cuban cigars and expensive brandy clung to him, as well.

"Did you just wake up?" she asked, looking him up and down.

"Of course I just woke up. It's the middle of the night."

"But how did you know I needed you?"

"I don't know." Ryan raked a hand through his hair. "I was having trouble sleeping, because I kept worrying you were going to read me the riot act for leaving you to smoke cigars with Max. So I decided I'd rather face you now than in the morning."

She hugged him again. "Well, whyever you're here, I'm glad."

He eyed her suspiciously. "Yeah, I can tell."

"Listen, Ryan, here's the thing." She pulled him over to the bed, pulling him down to sit beside her. "I've got it all figured out, but now we have to decide what to do with it."

"What are you talking about?"

"My father...and your uncle. It seems my father borrowed money from Max. Out of the frying pan and into the fire. He paid back the accounts he stole from to cover his first mistakes, but then he got even bigger debts, this time to the mob."

"How do you know this?"

"Joey." She paused, running a hand through her bangs. This was all still so confusing. "He was really very nice about it. Do you think he's going to get into trouble for telling me?"

Ryan sighed. "He would if Max found out. I'm not telling him. Are you?"

"No way." She sighed. "But, Ryan, what do we do next? Do we tell the police? Do you think I should rat on my own father?"

"I don't know, Lockett." He set an arm around her shoulders. "You know what I would do. But, sweetie, it's not like you really have any more than you did before. There's still no proof."

"I know." She rose, beginning to pace. "This is driving me crazy, Ryan. I can't take this much longer. To know what he did, and not be able to stop him, or turn him in... It's terrible."

"So if you had the evidence, you would turn him in?" Ryan asked.

Lockett took a deep breath. "I think I would have to. I think that's the only honorable thing to do. It doesn't matter that he's my father. It matters that he cheated people. And not just me. All his clients whose money he stole to put into Seaboard Development. They deserve to know where their money went." Ryan was still silent, so Lockett was forced to ask, "You think this is the right thing to do, don't you?"

"Yes," he said softly. "I think it's the only thing to do."

And he smiled at her, as if he were proud of her and her choices. It didn't take away the hurt at knowing what her father was. But it still felt really good to bask in that smile.

"Okay." She began to pull clothes on over her nightgown. "So now what? I vote we get out of here before Uncle Max wakes up and realizes we're on to him."

"I agree."

"You do?" Lockett smiled up at him. "Us agreeing—what a nice change of pace."

"Yeah," Ryan said easily, tucking in his own shirt. "I could get used to this."

As the two of them got dressed, Ryan began, "I've been thinking about this, Lockett. We've overlooked something. And I think that's the answer to where we look for evidence."

"What?" she asked quickly. "Where?"

"Stanford."

"Stanford?" She glanced over in surprise. "What about him?"

"Remember, you told me he got a promotion right before this all started. This is what I think. Your ex-fiancé stumbled onto something incriminating," he said with growing conviction. "I think he took it to your father and said, 'Hey, Elliot, I know what you did, and I'm going to talk unless you pay me.'"

"Blackmail," Lockett concluded. "It fits. Oh, Ryan, this is even worse. My dad was getting blackmailed on one side and pressured from the mob to repay his loans on the other. No wonder he was so crazy!"

"Lockett, it's no excuse," he said softly. "I'm sorry— I know you want to make it better. But it's his own fault."

"Yeah." She nodded. "I know that."

Ryan kissed her on the forehead, and held her for a long moment. "Okay, kiddo, so what do we have?"

"Stanford demanding money from Daddy to keep quiet . . ."

"And Elliot with no money to pay crafty Stanford— he was in dire straits already. So what did he do?"

Lockett knew what this was leading to. The final betrayal. "He offered me instead."

"Well, you and your trust fund, anyway. And bingo, the mystery is solved. Why did Elliot want you to marry Stanford so desperately? Because if he didn't, Stanford was going to expose all his dirty little deals." Ryan narrowed his eyes. "Although, considering the minuscule amount in your trust fund, your ex-fiancé is a pretty cheap date."

"Better than nothing, I guess." Lockett's lips curved in a rueful smile. "And he did get me in the bargain."

"Such a deal." He hugged her tight, affecting a brighter tone. She knew he was trying to cheer her up, and she was willing to go along with it. It was hard to stay depressed all the time, even if she had been played for a fool by everyone she knew. "You know," Ryan declared, "you look great in the middle of the night." He fastened his lips to the curve of her neck, edging her backward into the bed. "A real bed, you, me, a complete puzzle, nobody mad at anybody for a whole five minutes. Why waste it?"

"Oh, I wish we could," she whispered.

He stilled, his lips still inside her collar. "Why can't we?"

"Because we have to get out of here. Ryan, I really think we need to go, tonight. Joey left me some car keys." She dangled them under Ryan's nose. "I think maybe he's afraid Max will find out we know about the loan and try to keep us from leaving. Now if we only knew what car the keys fit."

Ryan's hand closed over the keys. "My car," he said tersely. "Joey must've brought it up here. I called him from the commuter station and told him to pick up my bike. He must've dropped that off and brought the car. I didn't tell him to do that. Joey is getting awfully helpful in his old age."

"You have a car?" But he was already pulling her off the bed, heading out the door, dragging her along behind him. "And the motorcycle, too? Are you telling me I have been riding on a bumpy bike and you had a car all the time?" she asked lightly.

"Shh," he whispered. "Do you want to get out of here or not?"

To Lockett's complete amazement, he led her to a huge, detached garage that must've housed forty vehicles. It was more like a new car lot than a garage.

"Don't tell me," she said when Ryan ushered her into a sleek black sports car. "This can't be yours."

"Why not?" he returned.

"Where would you get the money for something like this?" Ryan had never had two cents to rub together. She knew that firsthand. And he'd told her he worked as a caddy or something the one time she'd gotten anywhere near getting an answer. How did caddies afford fancy sports cars?

"I have my sources." But then he put the car in gear and blasted off into the wilds of Wisconsin.

Lockett settled into the racy leather seat, preparing herself for a long drive. Sometime soon, she hoped to stay in one place for more than a few hours. This on-the-run stuff sounded exciting, but it left a lot to be desired.

"Lockett," Ryan said after a moment. "Where do you want to go this time?"

She considered for a moment. It was awfully nice to be consulted for once, instead of just lugged around like a piece of baggage. And she had an answer all ready, too.

"Well, I really think you're right— Stanford is the crucial link here. I don't know how best to confront him, but if he was blackmailing my father, I just know he's got the evidence we need under lock and key. So," she finished up, "I think his house in Evanston is our best bet. I know Stanford pretty well, and I think he'd keep whatever it is he's holding over my father's head in his safe at home, where he can take it out and look at it from time to time. Gloat, you know."

Ryan flashed her a wary glance. "Don't tell me you know where his safe is, too?"

"Well, yes, of course."

"All these people just volunteer to show you where they keep their valuables?"

"I'm a very easy person to trust," she told him with a certain air of mischief. "At least for some people. It just so happens that Stanford kept my engagement ring in that safe. He proposed, and then he popped it open to show me the ring."

"I've never seen you wearing an engagement ring."

"Well, he keeps it in the safe." She tried not to sound defensive. "It's a family heirloom, and he didn't want me to lose it."

"Oh, yeah. He trusts you big time."

"I saw the safe, didn't I? I even know the combination. It's the name of his dog." She sniffed. "Some people are so predictable. Whereas others keep all sorts of secrets."

"I have my reasons."

"Ha! You just like keeping me in the dark. Send the woman off while you discuss business over cigars." She crossed her arms over her chest and watched the dark, shadowy scenery whizzing by outside her window. "How insulting."

"Okay, Lockett," he said grimly, purposely changing the subject. "So we're going to visit Stanford and bust into his safe. But it's four o'clock in the morning. Do you want to go get him out of bed, too?"

"So you're saying we should wait until morning?"

"I'm saying we should wait till he leaves the house."

She pondered that. "Okay. I think you're right."

"Do you want to sit on the street outside his house till he goes away? Or do you have some other suggestion of how to spend the next few hours?"

Honestly. He was making this so difficult for her. One decision, one moment to be in charge and call the shots, and it required the resolution of endless details.

"Well..." she said softly. Her gaze skittered over to catch his. "I do know a place with a real bed, you, me, a complete puzzle, nobody mad at anybody for a whole five minutes..."

Ryan went very still. Lockett smiled.

"Where is it?" he asked gruffly.

"Clybourn Street. Do you know where that is? It's where my store is. Locketts and Lace. I have an apartment upstairs. An apartment nobody knows about."

He slammed the accelerator all the way down.

It was already starting to get light by the time they got to her store. Locketts and Lace was a pretty little boutique in a one-hundred-year-old building with a turret on the corner and a balcony in front.

Lockett had fallen in love with it the first time she'd seen it. She'd had it painted and remodeled, and she'd turned it into a shop full of hankies and doilies, draped with exquisite dresses and vests made out of old table linens. She specialized in reproductions of Victorian gloves and hats, with a tiny enameled box or a velvet pillow here and there. And, of course, lockets. There were lots of lockets.

Rich women loved her store. She was doing a land-office business.

The truly weird thing was that no one in her family had ever cared to know much about her shop. And none of them, not even Beatie, knew that Lockett kept an apartment, a pied-à-terre, above the shop. None of them, not even her sister, knew how important that store was to Lockett.

And now she was suddenly very shy to share her special place with Ryan.

"Pretty," he commented. His gaze skimmed the shelves and the racks. "I saw it from the outside before, once I was keeping an eye on you, but I'd never have guessed how beautiful the inside was."

"It is beautiful, isn't it?" She held her head high, sweeping through to the storeroom in back, brushing the crown of a straw hat dripping with silk flowers, ruffling the sleeve of an embroidered gown that looked just right for an Edwardian tea party.

"I feel a little out of place, I have to admit," he whispered. "As if I might break something if I touch it."

"It won't break. A lot of this stuff has lasted a hundred years." With one foot on the stairs up to her apartment, she smiled at him. "I don't think one desperado can wreck hundred-year-old linens."

He caught her from behind, and he pulled her back off the steps, up against his body, very close in his arms. He bent his head down until his lips grazed her ear. "There's something to be said for desperadoes, Lockett."

She shivered in his arms. She did want him, no question there. But she needed him, too.

"I like that dress," he told her in that same, sexy, husky voice that tickled her nerve endings. "The one you were holding. It reminds me of you, kind of innocent and proper, but something special and unique. I always find myself wanting to know what's going on under the lacy, pristine surface."

Ryan had never spoken to her with words like this— all sentiment and flowers. She loved it.

He rubbed his cheek softly against hers. "You know, I thought you were absolutely gorgeous when I saw you in your wedding dress. All that hoopla. But you should've worn something like this. Simple. Elegant. You."

Her breath was stuck somewhere below her throat, and it only got more constricted every time his lips nibbled her neck.

She felt herself melting, relaxing, giving in to the bewitching idea of making love with Ryan here among her linens and lace, again and again. Her secret place. And she was sharing it with Ryan.

He spun her around. His long, clever hands bracketed her face.

"I love your store, Lockett," he whispered. "And...I love you, too."

"But—I thought you weren't sure."

He kissed her neck, licked her ear, bit gently on her lobe. "There's no way I could not love you."

And then he covered her mouth with his, delving deep, plunging inside with such delicious heat and urgency that she could barely stand. As she faltered, he swung her easily up into the hard circle of his arms, cradling her next to his chest. His eyes held her as securely as his arms.

"On the train, you said you always loved me, but you weren't sure it was enough. It's enough for me."

"It's plenty," she said, offering him a hazy smile. She tangled one arm around his neck, and traced his lips with a finger from her other hand. "Kiss me again."

His mouth was hard and insistent, as if he were impossibly greedy and couldn't get his fill. She had always loved his mouth, loved the way he felt, the way he tasted. But this wasn't enough.

Breathless, Lockett broke away. "Let's go upstairs," she told him. "Now. I want you to make love to me. This time, it will be Ryan and Lockett. Not kids anymore. We'll go with our eyes open. We'll know exactly what we want."

"Eyes open," he echoed.

And then he strode up the stairs, and he kicked open the door.

Chapter Fifteen

Runaway Rapture

He deposited her on the first soft thing he came across—a curved white sofa in the living room.

"There's a bed," she tried. "Back there."

"I can't wait that long."

He tumbled onto the couch with her, pulling off her clothes, ripping at his own, driving her crazy with the urgency of his need.

"Slow down. I can't breathe." She tried to catch his head with her hands, to hold him, but he was moving too quickly, sliding his lips over her shoulders and her neck, her collarbone.

"No," he said plainly. "I've waited too long. It's got to be fast."

Her head fell back. She arched into him. She was on fire, she was hungry, and she needed to feel his hands, his mouth, everywhere.

He framed her breasts, cupped one in each hand, teasing her nipples, rubbing the hard little peaks with his thumbs. She was already moaning with pleasure, but she couldn't seem to stop.

Somehow this had escalated way out of control the moment he'd kicked open the door. There was no turning back now, not even a chance to breathe or to form a coherent thought.

Each new place that he touched seemed to burst into hotter, more intense flames, until she was rocked, devastated by the onslaught of sensation. She made a funny little whimper as his mouth moved to her breast, covering one taut nipple, biting down gently. Reckless, she ran her hands down his long, strong back, urging him closer. His skin felt so alive, so vibrant, under her fingers. She pulled at him, angled a leg around him, trying to push him faster.

Her body felt slippery and hot, so hot. She pressed her hips against his, trying desperately to fit the pieces together more completely.

But he held back the one thing she wanted the most.

"I thought you were in a hurry," she said raggedly. "Ryan, please. I can't take much more."

"Oh, yes, you can." His smile was wicked above her. He bent to nip her shoulder, to tease the peak of her breast with one flick of his tongue.

And all the time he moved against her, creating a tantalizing, slow, sweet rhythm, letting her know exactly what was beyond her grasp.

"Now," she begged.

"No."

"Now."

"No," he said, making her tremble from the inside out.

But she wasn't going to sit back and let him make all the rules, not when she was writhing with need, when she had long since gone past the point of simple desire.

This was a headier, hungrier place, a place where his holding back was no longer an option.

She slid to the outside, almost off the couch, knocking him over onto his side. And before he could stop her, she rolled on top.

She smiled. He was flat on his back underneath her. He was at her mercy.

Astride him, in command, she leaned forward, bracing herself on his shoulders, brushing his chest with the ends of her hair. The darkness of his tanned skin and his flat nipples stood out in sharp relief against her golden hair.

It was an erotic, fascinating picture.

Under her, still teasing her, she could feel the hard, smooth man. Closing her eyes, she slid closer.

Then Lockett opened her eyes. Sweat glazed Ryan's brow, but his beautiful green eyes, thick-lashed, sparkling with mystery, held her fast. She read the challenge there. Would she dare?

Yes, she would.

"Now," she said with a sense of complete and utter power. She slipped down with one slick stroke, taking him deep inside.

"Ryan," she said. "Ryan."

He grabbed her hips, held her immobile for a long moment, and then arched up into her with one last, powerful stroke.

"Heaven," she murmured.

She collapsed onto his chest. His lips brushed her temple as he caught one finger in a tendril of her hair.

She realized then that she had called him Ryan, not Tony, even at the moment of absolute truth.

She knew why. She wasn't making love with the boy anymore. She had found the man.

MORNING LIGHT streamed in brightly, coming from the window over the balcony. Lockett squinted her eyes at it, bracing herself on the warm, hard chest underneath her.

"Morning? Already?" she murmured.

Her body felt all woozy and tingly. Every muscle she moved sent back remembered sparks. Lockett smiled. She hadn't felt this good in a long, long time.

Trapped under her, Ryan was completely naked and once more at her mercy. With his head pushed into the curve of the couch, one arm fast around her, half her body sprawled on top of him, he had somehow managed to stay deeply asleep.

She didn't blame him. It had been a tumultuous evening.

"Wake up," she whispered, dropping kisses on his chin. One hand snaked down his chest, past the hard plane of his hip, searching, teasing. "We have to go to Stanford's house, but first I know a wonderful way to wake up," she breathed in his ear.

But then she heard sirens, banishing any thoughts of a lazy, erotic morning. Loud, insistent sirens. And they sounded very close.

Flashing red lights reflected through the window. And then a very loud banging downstairs on the front door of her shop.

"Open up! Police!"

They both jumped to their feet, tumbling off the sofa. Lockett grabbed Ryan's shirt and shoved her arms into it, managing to cover herself as she stumbled out to the balcony overlooking Clybourn Street.

The voice from outside bellowed, "We know you're in there, Ryan. We've got your car."

Blinking into the sun, she said, "What's going on?"

But the street was full of police cars. Red dome lights flashed all the way up and down the block. As she struggled to take it all in, she saw uniformed cops, guns drawn, pointed at her.

Behind her, Ryan was pulling on his pants. "Stay back," she shouted. "Ryan, there's a million of them."

"Are you Lockett Kensington?" a man below her called in a no-nonsense voice.

"Ryan, hurry. You might be able to make it out the back—"

"No way," he said curtly. "I'm not going to leave you here."

"Are you Lockett Kensington?" the officer boomed again.

"Yes, yes. Don't shoot." She held up her hands. "There's nothing wrong here."

"Is the kidnapper with you? Is he inside?"

"There is no kidnapper!" she snapped. "What's wrong with you people?"

About twenty triggers pulled back.

"Lockett, be quiet, please?" Ryan commanded. "It's probably not a good idea to antagonize them."

Just then the door burst in. Before her very eyes, Ryan, without even the dignity of a shirt or shoes, was thrown facedown on the floor and handcuffed.

"Don't hurt him," she cried. "He wasn't resisting. He wasn't doing anything. Don't you people listen? He didn't kidnap me—he saved me."

"Your family will be here for you shortly, ma'am," one of the policemen said kindly. "Maybe you'd like to get dressed."

"My family? But don't you see—my father is the one who should be carted off. He's the criminal."

THE PRINCESS was once more imprisoned in her tower.

Her parents had carried her off, amid all kinds of silly chatter about brainwashing. The implication was clear—if she didn't cooperate, they'd let Ryan rot in jail, and send her off to the loony bin. So far, they hadn't even let her speak to the police or the FBI. They said she wasn't emotionally stable enough.

Right now Elliot and Marjorie Kensington were carrying on a press conference downstairs in the garden, complete with Lockett's odious ex-fiancé at their side. She was just sure they were waxing all teary about their daughter's return, even as they knifed her in the back by pretending she was mentally unbalanced.

In fact, Lockett didn't have one ally in the house. Beatie had been shipped off on an extended vacation in Europe, poor girl. Lockett had every hope her sister would escape, too. Once Lockett was out, with Ryan cleared, she promised herself she would go in search of her sister.

Her parents could lock their daughters in towers all they wanted, but that didn't mean the princesses had to cooperate. When the going got tough, princesses got going.

And this time, Lockett was on her way. Wearing jeans and a sweatshirt and some capable climbing boots, she blithely tossed a lamp out the new, unopenable window. And then she maneuvered herself out over the shards, over the sill and down the trellis.

Child's play, really.

She knew very well her parents and Stanford were occupied on the other side of the house, in the gardens, so she jumped down and ran to the front. These people were really not all that smart. There was her car, parked right where she needed it. The trusty key was under the mat, and Lockett blasted off to freedom.

Once again, they were making things easy for her. Since they had Stanford with them at the press conference, he obviously was not at home.

She didn't even bother to hide her car. Bold as brass, she left it on the driveway.

All she had to do was walk in the French doors to his study. She knew he never kept them locked; he'd told her so. Once she was in, his dog, a very nice springer spaniel named Daphne, came romping up to greet her.

"Hello, sweetheart," she said as the dog licked her hand. Some watchdog.

From there, it was only a few steps to the safe, where she punched in the letters D-A-P-H-N-E. How nice that Stanford loved his dog.

And, unbelievably, it was all there, neatly marked in Stanford's small, spare handwriting. Lockett riffled through. Very damning. One entire file detailed the Seaboard Development fiasco, including her ex-fiancé's helpful notations on which sums of money had come from where, so that all the clients Elliot Kensington had illegally transferred funds from were accounted for.

There was only one sheet of paper relating to the loan from Max Fiorin, but that was enough. Who knew mob kingpins made people sign documents spelling out the terms of their loan agreement?

"Thank you, Uncle Max," she said out loud.

And last, but not least, there was a suspiciously different file concerning her trust fund. In this one, all of Grandmother's millions were back where they belonged.

"Two sets of books," she whispered. "How very odd."

Although she was no whiz at reading legal gobble-dygook, she did manage to figure out that her grand-mother's assets were tied up tight, and that no one was allowed to touch them until after Lockett reached the age of thirty, or married, whichever happened first. There was no management involved. The money just sat there, collecting dust.

The other file, the one they'd snagged in her father's safe, had to be the fake. She didn't know why they'd needed to do it, but she guessed it fit in somewhere. Maybe it was all part of the plan to explain why her trust fund had had millions in it the day before she got married, but was reduced to almost nothing once her father and Stanford got their grubby mitts on it.

None of it mattered. She would leave it to better legal minds to figure it all out. She just wanted to turn it over, and fast, before anybody else discovered what she was up to.

Lugging all of Stanford's blackmail files, Lockett sat at his desk. She called the police station. She asked politely, "Can you tell me who Antonio Ryan's attorney of record is?"

It took them a few minutes, but somebody tracked down the information. And then Lockett lit out of Stanford Marsh's home, on a beeline to find one John Tennyson, attorney-at-law.

His office was small and rather dingy. Poor Ryan. He obviously couldn't afford a high-powered lawyer. Through the crack, she saw a thirtyish man in a feverish state of activity, thumbing through a pile of books on his desk.

She knocked tentatively on the door. "Excuse me? Are you Mr. Tennyson? Ryan's attorney?"

"Yes." Without looking up, he said, "If this is about an interview, we're not doing any at the moment."

"It's not." She barged right in and shut the door behind her.

"I'm pretty busy..." But then he chanced to look up. "Oh, my God." He stood abruptly. "You're Lockett Kensington. I've been trying to get a hold of you for the past twenty-four hours."

"I was imprisoned in a tower," she said flatly. "Don't bother to ask—it's not worth explaining. How soon can we bail Ryan out? I'll pay whatever it takes."

"Well, he hasn't been formally charged yet. I'm not sure he will be, but right now they aren't offering bail because of the seriousness of the crime involved, and because he's such a bad risk, given the, uh, fact that the two of you eluded authorities for quite some time." He smiled apologetically. "Ryan's pretty steamed about it. We've been lobbying hard to get them to either charge him or release him. So far, no luck."

"There has to be a way to get him out." She brandished her armload of files. "What about this stuff? It will take you a while to sort through, but it shows what was really going on, and why my father yelled kidnap when it was no such thing. There are little notes on the files explaining what they are. It should be plenty to get Ryan released."

He was already scrambling to look in the folders. "This is great," he murmured.

"Okay, so when can you get Ryan out?"

"Hopefully, I can get somebody at the U.S. attorney's office to go over this information within a few hours." He gestured to a seat. "Do you want to wait? So you don't get stuck in any more towers or anything?"

"Oh, that would be lovely." Her heart leapt at the idea it could all be handled so simply, that she and Ryan could be back together within a few short hours. She sat down and then stood again immediately. "But maybe I should put on something a little nicer before I see him."

But Ryan's lawyer was too busy poring through ledgers and scribbling on a legal pad to hear her.

"I meant to tell you..." She hesitated. "I would really like to pick up Ryan's legal fees." She gazed around at the less-than-prepossessing surroundings. "And if you'd like to bring in some help, you know, F. Lee Bailey or anything, well, that would certainly be all right."

"Excuse me?"

"The legal fees. I would like to pay them."

"Oh, that's not necessary." He flushed uncomfortably. "Ryan is taking care of it."

"But I know he doesn't have very much money, and since this is all my fault, really, I'd like to—"

Mr. Tennyson's hairline seemed to recede before her very eyes. "What do you mean? This is a joke, right?" He laughed nervously. "I mean, Antonio Ryan not having any money? Since when?"

"Well..."

"Look, I know my office doesn't look like much, but Ryan didn't come to me out of lack of funds. It's loyalty." He smiled. "We caddied together at the Old Scotsman's Club, way back before he turned into, you know, *the* Antonio Ryan."

"*The* Antonio Ryan?"

"The golf course designer. You mean, you didn't know?"

"I seem to be the last to find out most things," she said slowly. "He told me he had something to do with golf courses, but I thought he was kidding. Are you telling me that Ryan is good at this golf course designing thing?''

"The best. He owns a company, has a bunch of employees, wins awards, gets asked to design special courses for resorts. I mean, there aren't that many people who design golf courses—'' He broke off awkwardly. "I'm really surprised you didn't know."

"So," she said smartly, "am I."

And with that, Lockett wheeled on her heel and left. When Ryan got out of jail, she was going to be waiting for him.

And she was going to kill him.

IT TOOK LONGER than his lawyer thought. Sometimes the wheels of justice ground exceeding slow.

But by the time another day dawned, the U.S. attorney's office in Chicago had announced that they would not be proceeding with any charges related to kidnapping, although they were looking into allegations of wire fraud and other financial misdeeds. They were also seeking indictments for a variety of charges relating to filing false police reports and obstruction of justice.

As Ryan walked out of the federal courthouse, Elliot Farnham Kensington III, R. Stanford Marsh, and one Max Fiorin were going in to be arraigned themselves.

Lockett was waiting at the bottom of the steps, wearing a tight magenta suit, her hair slicked into a chignon and hidden under a huge hat. She was worried that she looked like she belonged on a soap opera in the role of a viper woman... but she was making a statement.

Cameras flashed, news crews crowded around, and her father and his lawyer made the big climb up the stairs. She hadn't realized she would have to see him here. For some reason, that was a lot scarier than seeing Ryan this morning.

As she watched, Elliot Kensington said a few words to his lawyer and then crossed to see her. She hadn't been sure he would bother.

"Lockett," he said softly. "Are you all right?"

She chewed off a bit of her immaculate lipstick. "Yes, Dad. I'm fine."

"I'm glad to hear it."

She wasn't at all sure she believed him. She gripped her purse and looked at his shiny black shoes.

"I'm sorry, Lockett," he whispered. "I didn't mean to... Things didn't turn out..."

She lifted her chin. "You used me...your own daughter. You ought to be sorry."

He gave her a twisted smile. "I'm almost relieved it's over. I was in a tight spot."

"I know."

And with that he backed away slowly, rejoining his lawyer, entering the courthouse.

Funny, but she didn't even mind so much anymore. She was still frozen on the issue of her father. Maybe later, much later, she would forgive him. But not yet.

Meanwhile, she had Ryan to think of. Looking very dashing in a beautifully cut black suit with a crisp white shirt and tie, her ex-husband skipped down the stone steps quite jauntily, headed right for her. He had cut his hair.

Lockett felt a definite pang. She wanted his hair back. She wanted him back, barefoot and shirtless, all sweaty with love and exertion.

Closer now, he smiled with the lighthearted, reckless charm that had once taken her breath away. He held out his arms.

She waited until she got all the way down to her. And then, in front of all those reporters and well-wishers, she smacked him.

He jumped back. "What was that for?"

"That was for letting me believe you were exciting and dangerous and *poor*," she said coolly. "I was willing to forgive all those things, and they weren't even true. I thought we were beyond secrets, Ryan. Or should I call you Mr. Golf Course? Mr. Ducati Handmade Italian Motorcycle. Mr. Ferrari. What a dope I was."

Holding on to her huge hat, Lockett turned and walked away. Away from the man in the dashing black suit. Away from the only man she had ever loved.

ON THE SECOND FLOOR, above the store called Locketts and Lace, the princess stared out her window into the pale blue, cloudless sky of a summer evening.

But who saw the sky? She was miserable. She was dying for Ryan.

Since she'd left him on the steps of the courthouse two days ago, she hadn't seen or heard from him. The only news she'd had was from Beatie, who had arrived home from Europe with a new boyfriend in tow. He was Swedish and blond and very cute, and he had helped her escape from the tour she was stuck on.

One more princess on the loose.

Lockett moved away from the balcony window. Okay, so she'd screwed up. She shouldn't have slapped him. She should have politely asked what in the hell he thought he was doing with this secret identity nonsense, and then she should've slapped him. Or maybe just killed him.

But it didn't matter anymore. She was willing to forgive him. But first she had to be asked, nicely.

First she had to at least *see* him.

One more day and she was going to break down and call John Tennyson, or maybe even Joey Fiorin, to see if they knew where her mysterious lover had gotten to.

Meanwhile, her attention was distracted by some sort of disturbance out on the street. She heard honking and shouting. Listlessly, she wandered over to the window to see what the matter was.

From out of nowhere the growl of a motorcycle broke through the noise. A man dressed all in black blasted into sight, riding not on the street, but up over the curb.

"Lockett," he cried from below her window. "Lockett!"

Her heart stood still.

She started to go to the balcony, to wave to him, to run to him, but something stopped her. The last time they did things this way, they ran away into the night and ended up at some lowly justice of the peace. And how long had they lasted together? Six months?

She wouldn't live her life that way again. It just didn't work.

"Lockett!" he called again. "I'm not leaving until you come out."

Rushing downstairs into the shop, Lockett grabbed a Victorian tea gown off the rack. As she raced back up the steps again, she was hopping out of her clothes and into the dress. So what if a few buttons were undone? She didn't care.

With a burst of speed, she jumped out onto the balcony and started to climb over the side. Passersby looked up in amazement.

"That woman is jumping off the balcony!"

But she had no fear. Ryan would catch her. He always had.

His motorcycle growled as he revved it. And Lockett clambered on behind him.

"Nice dress," he said with a smile.

"You're lucky I forgave you," she announced magnanimously.

"I know. I wasn't sure you would. So I decided to do something dramatic to catch your attention."

"You did." Her arms tightened around his waist, and she laid her cheek on the cool, worn leather of his jacket for just a moment. Never again would she let him out of her sight.

"Are you ready?" he asked, edging the bike off the curb through the crowd of onlookers.

"I'm always ready," she whispered into his ear. "But where can we find a justice of the peace at this hour?"

Once in a while, there's a story so special, a story so unusual,
that your pulse races, your blood rushes. We call this

TO HEAVEN AND BACK is one such book.

Danny Johnson doesn't know a good thing when he sees it.
Callie Moran is the perfect woman for him, but after losing his
fiancée a year ago, he can't look another beautiful woman in
the eye. Some celestial intervention is called for, and Jason and
Sabrina are just the pair to do it. Don't miss this companion to
HEAVEN KNOWS.

TO HEAVEN AND BACK
by
Tracy Hughes

Available in April, wherever Harlequin books are sold.
Watch for more Heartbeat stories, coming your way soon!

Take 4 bestselling love stories FREE

Plus get a FREE surprise gift!

HARLEQUIN

AMERICAN ◆ ROMANCE®

In Name Only

With the advent of spring, American Romance is pleased to be presenting three exciting couples, each with their own unique reasons for needing a new beginning...for needing to enter into a marriage of convenience.

Meet the reluctant newlyweds in:

#580 MARRIAGE, INCORPORATED
Debbie Rawlins
April 1995

#583 THE RUNAWAY BRIDE
Jacqueline Diamond
May 1995

#587 A SHOTGUN WEDDING
Cathy Gillen Thacker
June 1995

Find out why some couples marry first...and learn to love later. Watch for the upcoming In Name Only promotion.

HARLEQUIN®
AMERICAN ◆ ROMANCE®

IS BRINGING
YOU A BABY BOOM!

NEW ARRIVALS

We're expecting! Over this spring, from March through May,
three very special Harlequin American Romance authors invite
you to read about three equally special heroines—all of whom
are on a nine-month adventure! We expect each soon-to-be mom
will find the man of her dreams—and a daddy in the bargain!

So don't miss the next title:

> #579 WHO'S THE DADDY?
> by Judy Christenberry
> April 1995

Look for the New Arrivals logo—and please help us
welcome our new arrivals!

NA-1R

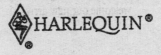

**Fifty red-blooded, white-hot, true-blue hunks
from every State in the Union!**

Look for MEN MADE IN AMERICA! Written by some
of our most popular authors, these stories feature some
of the strongest, sexiest men, each from a different state
in the union!

Two titles available every month at your favorite
retail outlet.

In March, look for:

UNEASY ALLIANCE by Jayne Ann Krentz (Oregon)
TOO NEAR THE FIRE by Lindsay McKenna (Ohio)

In April, look for:

FOR THE LOVE OF MIKE by Candace Schuler (Texas)
THE DEVLIN DARE by Cathy Thacker (Virginia)

You won't be able to resist MEN MADE IN AMERICA!

HARLEQUIN®

Don't miss these Harlequin favorites by some of our most distinguished authors!
And now, you can receive a discount by ordering two or more titles!

HT#25577	WILD LIKE THE WIND by Janice Kaiser	$2.99	☐
HT#25589	THE RETURN OF CAINE O'HALLORAN by JoAnn Ross	$2.99	☐
HP#11626	THE SEDUCTION STAKES by Lindsay Armstrong	$2.99	☐
HP#11647	GIVE A MAN A BAD NAME by Roberta Leigh	$2.99	☐
HR#03293	THE MAN WHO CAME FOR CHRISTMAS by Bethany Campbell	$2.89	☐
HR#03308	RELATIVE VALUES by Jessica Steele	$2.89	☐
SR#70589	CANDY KISSES by Muriel Jensen	$3.50	☐
SR#70598	WEDDING INVITATION by Marisa Carroll	$3.50 U.S. $3.99 CAN.	☐
HI#22230	CACHE POOR by Margaret St. George	$2.99	☐
HAR#16515	NO ROOM AT THE INN by Linda Randall Wisdom	$3.50	☐
HAR#16520	THE ADVENTURESS by M.J. Rodgers	$3.50	☐
HS#28795	PIECES OF SKY by Marianne Willman	$3.99	☐
HS#28824	A WARRIOR'S WAY by Margaret Moore	$3.99 U.S. $4.50 CAN.	☐

(limited quantities available on certain titles)

	AMOUNT	$
DEDUCT:	10% DISCOUNT FOR 2+ BOOKS	$
ADD:	POSTAGE & HANDLING	$
	($1.00 for one book, 50¢ for each additional)	
	APPLICABLE TAXES*	$_____
	TOTAL PAYABLE	$_____
	(check or money order—please do not send cash)	

To order, complete this form and send it, along with a check or money order for the total above, payable to Harlequin Books, to: **In the U.S.:** 3010 Walden Avenue, P.O. Box 9047, Buffalo, NY 14269-9047; **in Canada:** P.O. Box 613, Fort Erie, Ontario, L2A 5X3.

Name: _____

Address: _____ City: _____

State/Prov.: _____ Zip/Postal Code: _____

*New York residents remit applicable sales taxes.
 Canadian residents remit applicable GST and provincial taxes.

HBACK-JM2